Being an author has always been **Therese Beharrie**'s dream. But it was only when the corporate world loomed during her final year at university that she realised how soon she wanted that dream to become a reality. So she got serious about her writing, and now she writes the kind of books she wants to see in the world, featuring people who look like her, for a living. When she's not writing she's spending time with her husband and dogs in Cape Town, South Africa. She admits that this is a perfect life, and is grateful for it.

Also by Therese Beharrie

Tempted by the Billionaire Next Door
Surprise Baby, Second Chance
Her Festive Flirtation

Conveniently Wed, Royally Bound miniseries

United by Their Royal Baby
Falling for His Convenient Queen

Billionaires for Heiresses miniseries

Second Chance with Her Billionaire
From Heiress to Mum

Discover more at millsandboon.co.uk.

FROM HEIRESS
TO MUM

THERESE BEHARRIE

MILLS & BOON

Published in Great Britain 2019
by Mills & Boon, an imprint of HarperCollins*Publishers*
1 London Bridge Street, London, SE1 9GF

© 2019 Therese Beharrie

ISBN: 978-0-263-07988-3

MIX
Paper from
responsible sources
FSC™ C007454

This book is produced from independently certified FSC™ paper
to ensure responsible forest management.
For more information visit www.harpercollins.co.uk/green.

Printed and bound in Great Britain
by CPI Group (UK) Ltd, Croydon, CR0 4YY

For Grant, who sees me when I can't see myself.

I love you.

CHAPTER ONE

A POUNDING WOKE her up.

At first Autumn Bishop thought it was a dream. She'd gone to bed with one hell of a headache. Unsurprisingly: she'd spent a weekend away with her parents and sister, dealing with family drama, and had then driven six hours back to Cape Town.

The familiar throbbing had come shortly after she'd arrived at home. Right on time. Her head always ached when she was far enough away from her family to brood about how different she was from her sister. And how those differences made her feel like a failure.

When she heard the pounding, she thought it was that. Perhaps the pounding headache had manifested into a drumming. But then she heard a shrill ringing, and she woke up fully. Throwing the covers off, she ran to the front door, her stomach dropping when she opened it to Hunter Lee.

Her stomach kept free-falling as her eyes swept over him. His brown hair was wild, a sign that he'd let the wind style it. The strong features of his face were tight, as if someone had attached them to a string at his nose and pulled, forcing everything to be drawn to the centre of his face. Even the muscles of his shoulders—his chest, his entire body—were tense.

Something about it sent a wave of emotion, of awareness through her. When that wave collapsed, a second one of nausea replaced it.

'What is it?' she asked. 'What's wrong?'

'Everything.'

His voice, usually steady and strong, was hoarse, the word cracking. A part of her wanted to turn on her heel and climb back into bed; another, more forceful part spurred her forward. Before she knew it, her arms were circling around his significantly larger body.

She wasn't sure why she was hugging him. They'd avoided this kind of contact since they'd made the transition from lovers to friends a year before. Besides, he wasn't the kind for contact, unless in affection, and in private. But her instinct had been to comfort him. And, though she would never admit it aloud, to comfort herself at seeing him this way.

She drew back and took a deliberate step away from him.

'What happened?'

He stuffed his hands into his jeans pockets. Her eyes automatically followed the movement, and she shoved away a kick of appreciation. It didn't matter that his legs—those powerful, strong legs—deserved appreciation. Now was not the time.

'Can I come inside?'

His voice was steadier.

'Of course,' she said, opening the door wider.

Two things happened then. One, she held her breath, not wanting to get a whiff of his cologne. The smell never failed to twist her insides, even after their break-up, and she'd become accustomed to not breathing it in when she was around him. Two was that a light breeze followed Hunter through the front door. It wasn't particularly cool— cool and summer in the Western Cape of South Africa rarely went together—but Autumn shuddered, her skin shooting out in gooseflesh. And suddenly she realised how she looked.

She was wearing a silk nightdress, a gift from her mother, since it was the first thing she'd found in her cupboard before falling into bed. She groaned softly. It wasn't demure, though she might have been able to ignore that if her breasts had played along. They currently were not, having reacted to the breeze, and, along with the silk material, she knew she'd give Hunter an eyeful if she turned around like that.

Not that it was something he hadn't seen before. It was just... Autumn liked boundaries. Preferred them, where he was concerned. Where *they* were concerned. So she closed the door and crossed an arm over her chest. She wondered how terrible it was that she was thinking about her breasts when he was clearly upset.

'This is an emergency, I'm assuming,' she said when she turned around, crossing her free arm over her chest as well.

'Yes.' It was all he said for what felt like for ever. Then his eyes sparked. 'Not so much that you can't put on something that makes you feel more comfortable.'

Her cheeks heated. Instead of giving him the sarcastic reply she truly wanted to, she nodded, and went to her room. She grabbed the first thing she found to cover up—ironically, the silk kimono that, for reasons only her mother and heaven knew, matched the nightdress—and slipped her feet into a pair of sandals.

When she returned, she found him on the patio.

'Still can't get used to this view,' Hunter said quietly as she stopped next to him.

She followed his gaze onto the city of Cape Town. When she'd moved out of her family home—the Bishop mansion, as some people liked to call it—she hadn't tried to find somewhere outside the city she'd grown up in to live. She'd merely been drawn to the Bouw Estate.

It had green fields that exploded with wildflowers; rolling hills beyond the fields; a river that surrounded the estate. The old manor and barn on the property had been renovated into what were now her home and her bakery, respectively. Every time she stood outside on the patio, at the top of the mountain that led out of Cape Town, staring down onto the city, Autumn thought that the Bouw Estate might not have been intentional, but it had been necessary.

'You didn't come here at...' She paused, frowning when she realised she hadn't seen the time. 'What time is it?'

'A little after eleven.'

So she'd had all of an hour's worth of sleep.

'You didn't come here at eleven at night to talk about this view.'

His eyes slid over to her, the brown of them a well of emotion, before his head dipped in a curt nod. 'You're right.'

'When am I not?' she muttered. She gestured to the outdoor table she'd lovingly selected when she'd furnished her house. 'Shall we?'

He nodded, pulled a chair out and stepped back. With a sigh, she sat down, thanking him when he pushed it back in. She waited as he sat opposite her. A long silence followed. She used it to study him. To watch the emotions play over his face.

When his eyes met hers, she caught her breath, and wished she had something to drink to distract herself from how vulnerable all of this made her feel.

'I don't know how to say this,' he admitted eventually.

She let air into her lungs slowly. 'Just...get it out.'

He angled his head, as if accepting her suggestion, but didn't speak.

'Hunter.' She paused. 'Are you in trouble?'

He opened his mouth, and Autumn could almost see his lips forming *no*, but then he closed it again. Rubbed a hand over his face; took a deep breath.

'I am.'

She straightened. 'Yeah? You're in trouble?'

His eyes shone with an emotion she couldn't quite define. It disturbed her. She'd dated him for two years; they'd been friends for one more. She should be able to tell what he was feeling.

'Yes.'

After a brief moment of hesitation, she laid a hand on the one he'd rested on the table. 'What's going on?'

He took a breath, then exhaled sharply, his gaze lowering.

'I'm a father.'

'What?'

'I'm a father.'

She tilted her head, tried to process. But she couldn't. Her headache had dulled to something bearable, but it felt as if her mind had fallen out of her ear with that head tilt.

'I'm sorry, I thought you said—' She moved her head again. 'Did you say—?'

She broke off, told herself the question was ridiculous. He didn't say he was a father. He didn't say it twice. No. *No.* This was Hunter she was talking to. The man who'd gone quieter and quieter whenever she'd talked about their future together. The man who'd started pulling away from her long before they'd ended things because he'd realised he didn't want children.

There was no way that man, *this* man, was a father.

She let out a small laugh. 'You know…' she lifted her hand, though she didn't have any reason for doing it '… I thought I heard you say you're a father. Which is ludicrous, right?'

'It is,' he agreed quietly.

Relief burst in her chest as if it were a diva arriving at a party.

'Oh. Well, then, what is it? Because—'

'But it's true, Autumn.'

The diva was assassinated. The party turned into a funeral.

'Huh?' she said, inelegantly. 'What? No. You're not a father. You're… You're *you.*'

He inclined his head in both acknowledgement and acceptance, then folded his arms. 'I know. I responded in the same way,' he told her after a moment. 'I didn't believe it when she told me at first either.'

'She?' Autumn repeated through numb lips.

She tried to swallow, but the simple task seemed awfully hard. It was as if her throat had forgotten its entire purpose was to swallow. As if it, too, were stunned by what Hunter was telling her.

'She,' he confirmed with a tight nod. Though he had every right to be amused by the stupid question, Hunter spoke seriously. 'A woman I met a…a year ago.'

'A year ago.'

She was still so numb.

'After our… After.'

The words sounded distant, as if she were listening to him through a wall or through glass or perhaps under water. She blinked, trying to figure a way out, then lifted her hand to her hair, tucking it behind her ears in case it was obscuring the sound. But when he started speaking again, it was the same.

'I…was trying to deal with our break-up,' he said deliberately. 'It was hard, for both of us.'

But I didn't sleep with anyone else.

Her mouth almost said the words. Somehow, by nothing short of a miracle, it didn't.

'I wasn't dealing with it very well.'

Was she dreaming? Maybe she was having a nightmare.

'I went to the bar close to my house.'

She brought her hand to her legs under the table. Discreetly, she pinched her thigh, hard, but Hunter kept talking. She was awake.

'It was the night after we decided to end things. I started drinking. I didn't stop.' He paused. 'It was a drunken mistake. I… I made a mistake.'

Autumn sat back, her eyes sweeping over the frame of her house. She'd rebuilt it by herself, this house. It had been stately, impressive when she'd bought the estate. It had been falling apart, too, and she'd rebuilt it. The red brick outside, the balcony above them, all of that had been her.

When she'd struggled with her life, with trying so hard for people to see her, to love her, she came out here and looked at it. At what she'd built. It never failed to make her feel proud. Steadier.

Tonight, it couldn't anchor her.

She felt as if she were floating away. She wasn't quite sure where to, until she saw herself as a child, following her father around the Bishop Enterprises building. The home of their family empire. She watched as the child asked questions, was answered, but curtly, as if to brush her off. Summer, Autumn's twin sister's questions were answered patiently, though.

Then she was at home, at the Bishop mansion, listening to her mother talk about Summer. Autumn said the right things in response to her mother's concern. Waited patiently for her mother to ask about *her*. About Autumn. It never came.

Finally she saw her gangly frame at fifteen. She was standing outside her parents' house, waiting for her date to the school dance. When he arrived, he asked her where her sister was. Looked behind her—no, *through* her—to check for Summer...

The hurt that had informed her every action since those days flared again now. It asked why she wasn't enough. Why, even when she tried, people still didn't want *her*.

Even Hunter didn't want her. Of course, she'd known it when he'd agreed to break up. But they'd stayed friends. And she didn't have to try as hard with him. She felt the most like herself when she was with him. She almost felt like...like she *was* enough. As if she were the first choice.

Except she wasn't. She very clearly wasn't.

CHAPTER TWO

IT WAS AS if Hunter had been given X-ray vision and could suddenly see through flesh and bone. As Autumn sat staring at him, Hunter saw her hurt, the desire she had to scream at him. He saw how badly she wanted to run. From his news, from him. He wouldn't have blamed her.

He probably looked like a nightmare. He'd pitched up at her house at eleven at night, having got into his car almost as soon as Grace had left his place. He should have tried to get some sleep first, after he'd heard the news. He shouldn't have arrived at Autumn's house in a panic. But he doubted his ability to sleep. He probably wouldn't be able to for the foreseeable future, considering what it might hold.

What it *would* hold, he thought, Grace's words echoing in his ears.

He'd felt better when Autumn had opened the door, concern in her eyes. Something had clicked back in place when she'd put her arms around him. Now, that seemed like an appropriate punishment for coming to her with this.

Seeing how hurt she was, seeing her wanting to run, sent an unbearable ache through his body. Another appropriate punishment.

He'd thought he'd grown accustomed to her disappointment. Every day towards the end of their romantic relationship had been stained with its stickiness. She had never said it in so many words, but he'd sensed it. Every time he hadn't responded to her gentle probes about their future. Or when he hadn't added anything when she'd spoken about her dreams about having a family.

In truth, he'd been figuring out his answers. First for himself; then what he would give her. She wouldn't like them, despite the different ways he'd tried to phrase them in his mind. He'd spent too long trying to figure out what to tell her in the end, desperate for her not to have a low opinion of him.

But it had happened anyway, rightfully so. Just as it was happening now.

He could see it. In the tightness around her eyes. In the crease between her brows. More than that, he *felt* her disappointment, sharp and acute. Felt sharp and acute pangs in his chest as well. So he supposed he hadn't got used to it after all.

But no matter how much he wanted to, he couldn't say what she needed to hear: that he wanted to have a family with her. He couldn't. The desires she'd expressed when they'd been together had reminded him of how families broke. How siblings got sick. How losing them felt like losing everything in the world.

Each person involved in a family would get hurt. Would be irrevocably changed—or worse. He'd seen it with his own parents. With his own sister. He had no desire to put himself in a situation to feel that way again. Let alone with a woman he genuinely cared for.

And yet the first thing he'd done after their break-up was forget his responsible nature and get a woman pregnant. Then he'd come to her, to the woman he cared about, to tell her that their break-up had resulted in the very thing she'd wanted and he hadn't: a child.

The thing he now had and she didn't. What painful irony.

'Autumn,' he said when the silence extended long enough that even he, who was at home in silence, felt uncomfortable. 'Say something.'

Her lips parted, and for a split second Hunter remembered that they did that just before he would kiss her. But that memory was unwelcome, untimely. How could he think about kissing her when he'd just told her he was a father? When he'd just discovered he was a father?

He was a *father*.

Bile rose in his stomach. It was the same thing that happened whenever he thought about his own father. The man who'd put his feelings above his dying daughter's.

'Autumn,' Hunter said again, more insistently.

Autumn's eyes met his, and his breath did something strange at the gold that flickered in their brown depths.

'Are you okay?'

Her eyelashes fluttered. 'I— Yes.' She straightened. 'I'm okay.'

Her voice sounded strange too, as if someone had taken a hold of her voice box and were squeezing tightly.

'I'm sorry,' he said, because he needed to.

She closed her eyes, and he wanted to reach out. To brush a finger over the line where her dark lashes lay against the brown of her skin. To smooth the lines at her forehead.

Her eyes opened right then and before he could avert his own, their gazes locked. His heart stumbled in his chest, resulting in an uncomfortable beat against his chest bone. The *thump-thump* of his heart sounded in his ears, except he heard it as laughter, a mocking *ha-ha* at what he'd given up to ensure that what he'd told her tonight would never happen.

He forced his eyes away, onto the night lights of Cape Town. It used to comfort him once upon a time. Now it mocked him.

'You found out tonight?' she asked after some time had passed.

He nodded. Still, he couldn't look at her.

A voice in his head called him a coward.

'Grace, the woman I—' He stopped before he said something stupid. 'The mother of the child. She showed up at my place.'

'You didn't know before that?'

He shook his head.

'How old is the… How old?'

'Three months.'

She pursed her lips, though he'd caught the trembling long before she'd done it.

'I'm sorry,' he said again, eyes resting on her face now. She nodded.

'You're here because you're surprised.'

It wasn't a question.

'I'm here because—' he hesitated '—it's the first place I wanted to go. I needed to see you.'

Her tongue darted out, wet her lips.

'Why?'

He took a breath. 'You're my friend.'

'Not your only one.' She pushed back at some of the curls exploding over the silk band she wore. 'Certainly not the best one to deal with this.'

'No,' he agreed, but didn't say anything else. Couldn't. Because she was right.

She wasn't his only friend; not that he had many more. In fact, he had one more: his second-in-command, Ted. Most of his peak making-friends time—school, university—had been focused on other things.

Most of his school life he'd spent helping his parents take care of Janie, his baby sister, who'd had cystic fibrosis. *Ha!* a voice in his brain immediately said. He hadn't helped his parents take care of Janie; he'd helped his *mother* take care of Janie. His father had tapped out of her care early on, pronouncing himself too clumsy to help.

Hunter supposed he could understand that when it came to helping clear Janie's lungs of the mucus. The airway clearance therapy could have posed a problem for someone who was *clumsy.* But he didn't know how that prevented his father from helping to get Janie to her doctor's appointments. Or helping to keep her active. Getting her diet right. Doing anything, really, that would make Janie's life easier. Or make her feel as if she weren't a burden for the man who should have loved her unconditionally.

She was a bright kid who'd picked up on things without much encouragement. She'd noticed their father's lack of interest. Hunter had done everything he could to make up for it.

When she'd passed away, he hadn't wanted friends to know how much his life had changed. How his heart ached, all the time. How alone he felt. How…broken. He hadn't been able to tell his parents about it when they'd been fighting, all the time. So he'd stuck his head into books, reading about technology and then, after his parents' divorce, renewable energy. It had distracted him enough to survive. To thrive, even, if he thought about the tech business he'd started ten years ago during university.

But that had meant he'd spent his entire university career studying or working. And when his business had taken off, he'd spent his time making sure it stayed in the air. He'd hired Ted to help with that. He hadn't even thought about Ted when it came to this, though.

When he'd first seen Grace. When she'd told him about the baby. When she'd showed him pictures, and he'd seen a face that looked so much like Janie's his heart had flipped over in his chest. When she'd asked Hunter to help take care of the child.

No, for that, he'd immediately thought about Autumn.

'You're the only person who knows why this is…' He trailed off. He hoped she'd interrupt him. That she'd finished his sentence for him. She didn't. 'You're the only person who knows about my family.'

He didn't let her speak when she opened her mouth. Too late, he thought. Because if he didn't continue, he'd lose his courage.

'You have to help me take care of him.'

'What?'

'You... You have to help me. She wants me—needs me—to take care of him while she's finishing her articles at a law firm in Gauteng for the next three months.' His voice dropped to a whisper. A rasp. A sacrifice. 'I... I don't know how. Please, Autumn. Please, help me.'

Hunter's gaze felt like lasers pointed straight at her heart.

'I... I need a moment,' she said, and rose unsteadily to her feet. 'Coffee?'

He angled his head, looked down, and she chose to interpret the gesture as a *yes*. Though in all honesty, he could have shaken his head for *no* and she'd still have made him one. She was barely paying attention to him. She was only focusing on getting away from him.

She strode by him, through the glass sliding doors and past the stone-coloured furniture and yellow pillows she'd chosen because they made her happy. It had been the same reason she'd chosen the bright paintings on the walls, and why she'd stacked the bookshelves beneath them with romance novels.

Her kitchen looked much the same: splashes of colour that made her feel bright. Light. But the appliances were sleek and top of the range; the cupboards meticulously arranged for optimum usage; the pantry filled with every ingredient she needed for when she experimented with cakes or biscuits or cupcakes or desserts or, really, anything that tickled her fancy.

With unsteady fingers, she popped a pod in the espresso machine, put a mug where it was needed, pressed buttons and let the machine do its work. She frothed the milk while she waited, keeping her hands busy, avoiding the thoughts speeding through her mind. She placed the second mug in the machine with a new pod, added milk to the first, then did the same for the second when it finished. She set them both on a tray, fixed a plate of cookies she'd baked before she'd left for her parents' anniversary weekend, and set that on the tray.

She was ready to go out. Except she couldn't. She... didn't want to. Not yet. She braced her hands on her kitchen counter, lifting her head so she could see out of the window. She'd insisted the window be included when she'd been fixing up the house. Had insisted on the same thing when she'd built the bakery.

Usually, she'd take her coffee there in the mornings, about an hour before she'd have to be at the bakery, which was about the time the sun rose in summer. She'd watch the golden orb appear from over the hills in the distance; she'd see the faint blue of the river that ran along the edge of the Bouw Estate; and her eyes would rest on the fields of flowers she refused to cut, giving the estate a wild feeling she genuinely enjoyed.

Now, all she saw was blue-black darkness. It seemed like an appropriate representation of what was going on in her mind.

The rope that had been keeping her together since their break-up felt dangerously frayed. Which was in itself a danger, as pretending everything was fine was the only way she kept her insecurities at bay. The voices that told her it wasn't that Hunter didn't want a future, a family; it was that he didn't want one with her.

Look at how he spoke about his sister, the voice said. With such emotion. Respect, fondness, love. How could a man with so much to give not want to share that in a family?

She'd managed to dismiss it with Hunter's words. The truth, he'd assured her, was that he couldn't bear to repeat the painful experiences of his childhood. His sister had been sick, then died; his father had been physically present, but emotionally absent; and his parents had eventually divorced after Janie's death. How could she argue with that?

But she had. In silence, with herself, her insecurities

making damning arguments. Convincing arguments. Hunter's news made those arguments hard not to believe.

As she thought of it—that he had a child—a fresh bomb of pain went off inside her. She closed her eyes, held her breath, hoping it would stop the devastation. But it didn't, and she felt her insides be destroyed. Felt them crumble and lie disintegrated inside her.

As she let air into her lungs, she took the tray outside. Hunter sat exactly as she'd left him—stiff, staring out over the city—and she put the tray down in front of him.

She settled in with her coffee, but since her back was towards the city she was forced to look at Hunter. She sipped thoughtfully, waiting for him to look at her, ignoring the throbbing in her chest as she did. When he finally met her eyes, she tilted her head.

'How did it go?' she asked quietly. 'When she told you.'

He stared at her for a moment, then picked up his coffee. 'I…struggled.'

'So you were perfectly stoic, but freaking out inside.'

His mouth lifted. 'Pretty much.'

'You don't think she's lying?'

'No.'

The answer was quick and immediate, his voice hard. He was defending the woman, Autumn realised, though she didn't understand why the woman needed defending. She was only asking a question. But then, this was Hunter. Protecting what was his. And the woman was his now.

Her stomach twisted.

'She has no reason to lie,' he continued. 'And she showed me a picture. He looks…exactly like Janie did when she was a baby.'

'Oh.'

It was all she said; it was all the pain allowed her to say. All the other words that came to mind were selfish.

We could have had a child who looked like Janie. We

*could have done this together, and you wouldn't have had
to ask for help.*

'Is he sick?' she asked.

The cup he'd lifted crashed against the table as he set
it back down. 'I… I don't know.'

'You didn't ask?'

'No.'

'Hunter, why the hell wouldn't you ask if your baby
was sick?'

He didn't answer her, only looked stricken. Her heart
softened, though she refused to allow herself to show it.
Beneath the softness was a pain she hadn't known she
could feel.

He'd told her it was probably good he wouldn't have
children when he was a carrier of the CF gene. There were
zero chances then that he'd pass it down—the disease or
the gene. Now she was supposed to believe he'd forgotten about it?

'She would have told me if he was sick,' he said.

Autumn set her mug down, her own fingers trembling
too much for her to hold it.

'How would she have known? Newborns aren't tested
for CF here unless it's specifically requested. What?' she
asked defensively when he looked at her. 'I did the research.'

She continued so neither of them would dwell on why
she'd done it.

'Besides, Hunter, what do you know about this woman?'
She didn't wait for an answer. 'You met her twice. Once
the night you two had sex, and tonight. Now she's asking
you to take care of your child?'

'It's fair,' he said in a *back-off* voice.

'Of course it's fair,' she said, gritting her teeth. 'But you
don't know her. You have no idea what she would have told
you.' She paused. Saw his face. Sat back slowly. 'You've
already realised that.' There was barely a second before

she said, 'And you know you didn't ask because you don't want to know whether he's sick.'

Time passed. Seconds, minutes, she wasn't sure.

'You're right,' he said quietly. 'But I'll find out tomorrow.'

Tired now, she sighed. 'What's happening tomorrow?'

'She's dropping him off.' He picked up his coffee again, brought it to his mouth. When he was done, he looked her dead in the eye. 'Be there with me.'

CHAPTER THREE

THE SITUATION REMINDED him of his father.

Calvin Lee had expected Hunter to fill in where he'd lacked with Janie. Hunter knew it because his father would call him whenever he was expected to care for Janie on his own. Now, Hunter could see himself doing the same to Autumn. Treating her with that same selfishness. But he couldn't stop. Was urged forward by something he didn't understand.

'Hunter,' she said quietly, 'I can't see what either of us could possibly gain from me being there with you.'

Hunter thought about the hug she'd given him when he'd first arrived. He remembered the steadiness of her gaze, despite the news he'd told her. He could hear the concern in her voice, and, beneath it, a strength he desperately needed.

That was why he was here. He'd known she'd offer comfort, steadiness, strength. Because she was his friend. She cared about him. Even though he'd broken her heart by being unable to say yes to the family she wanted. Even though he'd seen some of the light in her eyes go out that day.

It had been part of what had spurred him to the bar the next night.

Her casual talks of a future and a family had forced him to face memories he'd been running from. Of him curling up to Janie as their parents argued in loud whispers outside Janie's door. Of distracting her when the arguments turned louder. Of almost being relieved that she hadn't been there any more when the arguments graduated into shouting.

And then, of the silence.

He couldn't imagine putting a kid through it. Through what Janie had suffered with her illness. Through what he'd suffered with his parents' marriage. Through what it felt like to have the possibility of carrying the cystic fibrosis gene hover like a noose around their necks. Or through having to make the hardest decision in his life about having a family because of it.

Now he was being forced to imagine it. He was being forced to face the fears.

He rubbed a hand over the back of his neck, over his face.

'I need you there,' he rasped, shame straining his voice. 'I don't know if I can do it.'

'Of course you can,' she said. 'You took care of Janie.'

The feeling he couldn't explain swelled, compelling him to beg.

'Please.'

The skin around her eyes crinkled in tension. She gave a curt nod. 'Fine. If it's that important to you, I'll go.'

'Thank you.'

He wanted to tell her she shouldn't have agreed. That she was being too nice to him; that he didn't deserve it. Neither did she. She deserved more than her ex-boyfriend and pseudo-friend asking this from her.

He left it at *thank you*.

'She obviously knew your name if she knew how to find you,' Autumn noted slowly, almost carefully after a bit. 'Or did you…?' She cleared her throat. 'Did you go back to your place?'

Heat curled around his neck. 'We, er, introduced ourselves when we met.' He didn't answer her question.

'So she knows your surname, too?'

He angled his head, trying to remember. The entire event was a little hazy. Another great example he'd set for his son.

His son.

'I think so.'

'Okay, then. So she looked you up on the Internet—'

'How do you know that?'

She gave him a look. 'If some guy I had a one-night stand with knocked me up and I knew his name, you can be sure I'd do an Internet search on him before finding him.'

His mug stopped halfway to his mouth and he just stared at her, his mind playing her words over and over again.

'If some guy I had a one-night stand with knocked me up...'

Purposefully, and much too violently, he brought the coffee to his lips, swallowing down the hiss when the still-hot liquid burnt his throat. But he relished the pain, since he deserved it for the criminal thoughts he'd had at Autumn falling pregnant with someone else's baby.

Selfish, selfish, selfish.

'Hunter?' she asked with a frown. 'Did you hear anything I said?'

'About the Internet search?'

She nodded.

'Yes. I probably should have thought about that.'

She studied him over her mug. 'I imagine you were… too surprised to think.'

'An understatement.'

'That bad?'

'It was fine,' he denied. Her eyebrow lifted. 'Shocking. It was shocking.'

'Enough for you to want to avoid the gene issue.'

He gritted his teeth, guilt flaring in his gut.

'Yes.'

'Enough for you not to realise what comes up when you do an Internet search for Hunter Lee.'

He didn't get what she was talking about for the longest moment, and then he shook his head.

'You don't mean—'

She wrinkled her nose. 'Afraid so.'

And he thought the situation couldn't get worse.

'Oh, no,' he groaned. 'She's seen me...' He couldn't finish the words.

'It wasn't that bad,' she said kindly.

'You have to say that,' he said, his jaw tightening, 'because you're the reason it's there.'

'Maybe,' she allowed. 'Or maybe it's there because you were having fun—'

'And you *filmed* it.'

'It was a social media challenge. I was supposed to film it.'

'I did it for you.'

'I appreciated it.'

'You utilised it.'

'A self-made billionaire doing a ridiculous dance for a social media challenge in my bakery?' She snorted. 'Damn right I filmed it. And look how amazingly it turned out.'

'For you,' he muttered darkly.

'I only used it to promote the bakery. I didn't sell your body parts on the black market.'

'It went viral.'

'Technically,' she continued, as if he hadn't spoken, '*I* didn't film it. Mandy did.'

'Yeah. We're no longer friends."

Autumn snorted again. 'Yeah, you two looked real enemy-like when you were bribing her to make you some cupcakes last month.'

He lifted a shoulder now, refusing to be taunted any further.

'And besides the ridiculous dance, you actually did something sweet, too.' Her eyes were happy. 'You took me into your arms, spun me around, dipped me right under a wedding cake and laughed.'

'You used that on your social media as part of a *#BakeryBoyfriend* campaign,' he accused.

'An icon was born.'

She grinned at him, and—damn it—his lips twitched. How could he resist that smile? The way it softened her eyes, lit up her face. The way it widened her full pink lips, and made her look years younger than she was.

It was enough to distract him from the fact that he was smiling. It felt like a feat. Hell, it was a feat. He didn't think he could feel anything other than the pure panic that had fuelled his actions until he'd started speaking with her. He shouldn't have been surprised. It had always been part of what had drawn him to Autumn, the way she made him feel. The way she made him forget.

When he'd met her at the wedding of one of his employees—which Ted had forced him to attend—he'd carried an anchor around with him. That anchor had tied itself to his ankle when he'd been six and his sister had been born with cystic fibrosis. It had grown heavier with each of his parents' arguments. With each disappointing prognosis from Janie's doctors.

When Janie had died, he'd just about sunk into the depths of the ocean from that anchor's weight. It had felt as if he'd been living under water from that moment forward.

Then he'd met Autumn, and he'd felt as if he'd been given air for the first time in almost two decades. Which was why he'd allowed their relationship to go on for longer than he should have. After a year of dating, she'd brought up their future together. The year that had followed had been a slow decline into the realisation that he couldn't have what he wanted with Autumn.

And he'd sunk right back into the ocean, reaching the floor of it when they broke up. He could almost understand why he'd looked for a lifeline in a random woman one night.

Not that it had worked. But it had brought him here again. With her. Predictably, he felt as if he was breathing again.

'The reason I bring it up,' Autumn said after a moment, 'is because she'll recognise me.'

His mind took some time to follow. 'Okay,' he said slowly. 'We're friends.'

'Do you think she's going to believe that?'

'She won't care.'

Her eyes had gone serious, and didn't waver from his. 'How sure are you about that?'

He searched her face. Saw what she needed to hear. 'One hundred per cent. There's nothing there beside this connection. The child.'

My son.

She didn't reply immediately.

'We'll see.'

'Autumn—'

'No, Hunter,' she interrupted with a tight smile. 'It's fine. If you think this isn't going to be a problem, then I'll help you get settled with the baby.'

For how long? He didn't ask it. She was giving him something here. Because of it, he felt stronger. More in control. Not like every force in the world had turned on him. So he would give her something, too.

'I'll call you tomorrow with the details.'

'Fine.'

'And I'll leave.' He stood, then stilled when she shook her head. 'What?'

'It's after midnight. You're physically and emotionally drained. You can't leave.'

His heart thumped. 'What's the alternative?'

'You stay here. In the spare bedroom,' she said wryly, when his mouth curved. He'd been planning on teasing her—heaven only knew why—and she'd caught him in it.

Instead, he said, 'I don't have to do that.'

'Yes, you do. I'm not interested in getting phone calls about your death.' Now she stood, picked up the tray. 'Down the passage, third door to the left.' Her eyes met his. 'I'll see you in the morning.'

CHAPTER FOUR

'Was that—? Did I see Hunter's car leave as I drove in?' Mandy asked as she walked into the bakery's kitchen the next morning.

Autumn's back was facing Mandy, so she allowed herself a quick breath and silent moan that Hunter hadn't left before her pastry chef had arrived at work. The rest of her team were already there, bustling in and out of the kitchen as they prepared for the breakfast rush that would soon begin. Autumn took another breath, then turned to Mandy with a smile.

'Yes,' she said brightly. 'He came over last night for dinner.'

Mandy's eyes narrowed. 'And he's only leaving this morning…?'

'We finished late, and we'd been drinking.'

'Hmm.'

Ignoring the disbelieving tone of the woman she considered a friend, Autumn quickly changed the subject.

'Give me highlights of what I missed this weekend. Then tell me how the Thompson wedding cake is coming along.'

'Good morning to you, too.'

'You were the one who came in here without a greeting.'

Mandy sent her a look, then launched into a concise report as she got ready for work. It had been that kind of efficiency that had helped Mandy work her way up to pastry chef in the six years since Autumn had started the bakery.

If she was honest, it felt like longer than that. Perhaps because she'd spent most of her childhood in the kitchen.

At first, it had been out of curiosity. She'd strolled down to the kitchen as the staff had been preparing for one of her parents' numerous parties, and had found herself hypnotised.

The pastries had drawn her attention almost immediately. She'd loved the colours and the smell of them; wondered at the skill and caution they were being decorated with. When one of the chefs had encouraged her to join in, starting her off slowly, patiently, she'd fallen in love with the creation process. And her parents' parties had become a way for her to participate in something she loved.

Later, it had been a chance to contribute to the functions in the only way she could. When she'd got older she'd realised the parties weren't only social events, but networking opportunities. Autumn didn't have Summer's business acumen, nor did she have the professional knowledge her father had invested into her sister. She couldn't talk potential foreign or domestic clients. She had no idea about the details of global merchandise and distribution.

So she baked. And when she left the kitchen, she charmed. And felt like a failure for it.

The smell of sweetness and coffee mingled with the faint freshness of the fields around the bakery usually comforted her. Today, her thoughts turned them sour. For a moment, they even tarnished the efforts she'd put into creating her bakery. The stained cement floors and wooden panelling looked dull. The natural light and countryside atmosphere she'd incorporated when renovating the barn felt kitschy. So did the neat rock-filled paths leading to the bakery; the gardens beyond it.

She'd thought it such a good idea. A cute bakery and café with great food and even better desserts a short trip outside Cape Town that felt like the middle of nowhere. Now, she doubted it. Her memories of growing up tended to do that.

They were always accompanied by the comparisons, starting much earlier than she could even remember. All she knew was that the visits to Bishop Enterprises hadn't been for her benefit. That her questions hadn't been answered in the same way that Summer's had. That the *there, there* nature of the response to her complaints to her mother had been meant to placate her. And that being sent to the kitchen to 'bake something' had been to distract her.

Any desire she might have had to join the family business had been stifled then already. But it had been well and truly shattered after her father's affair.

When Summer had found out Trevor Bishop had cheated, she'd pulled away from him. From Autumn and their mother, too. Autumn knew now that was because Trevor had asked Summer to keep the affair a secret, which had been a burden Summer had carried with her for years. Autumn had only discovered that this past weekend, at their parents' thirtieth anniversary.

It had upset her. Not because of her father's actions, though those weren't great. No, she was upset that Summer had kept the truth from her. And she was worried about what she'd done to bring that about.

Autumn was sure Summer didn't know she harboured a tiny bit of resentment towards Summer because their parents preferred her. But what if she *did* know?

Autumn had pushed the concerns aside during the weekend. It hadn't been important then anyway. Summer had needed her. Autumn might have been jealous of Summer—only a tiny bit—but she would be there for her sister.

She'd done something similar after her father's affair. Then, she'd thought her father needed someone to take over from Summer. Someone in the family who could run the family business. There had only been her, and she'd been so damn hopeful. But she still hadn't been good enough. In fact, her father had gone in an entirely different direction. He'd trained someone new; the man who had become Summer's husband. Then ex-husband. Now boyfriend.

The anniversary weekend had…complicated things.

The point was that her father had not once thought to focus on Autumn the attention he'd spent on Summer. Even when Autumn had asked if she could help, and how she could help, he'd told her she'd be better off elsewhere. She'd realised then that whatever she achieved in her life would have nothing to do with the Bishop family business. The Bishop money would get her foot in the door—and it had, with her father's start-up contribution to her bakery—but kicking it open would be up to her.

She had her doubts about that though. Still did, if she was being honest. Despite the success of her bakery, she worried something would happen that would take it all away from her. She'd do something wrong. Or people would finally realise she didn't know what she was doing. That she wasn't good enough. Her parents had believed that, hadn't they? They'd put Summer first, so they must have.

It didn't help that that was how things had gone with Hunter, too. Their relationship had been going well, and suddenly he'd been pulling away from her. She'd tried to talk away the insecurities as she usually did, but, like always, they were valid. Despite her trying to be a good girlfriend. A perfect girlfriend.

She was still doing it. Trying to be the perfect friend. What she couldn't figure out was why. She had nothing to prove to Hunter any more. They were friends because *he'd* approached *her* after their break-up. She hadn't been desperately chasing after him. In fact, she knew a friendship with him was a bad idea. And his situation with his *baby*? This request? It proved that. Because she knew it would bring her nothing but pain.

So why had she agreed to help?

'Autumn. *Autumn*.'

Autumn's eyes widened before they settled on Mandy. 'What?' she asked.

'Did you hear a word I said?' Mandy poured herself a cup of coffee. 'Or are you too busy thinking about Hunter?'

'I'm tired,' Autumn replied prudishly. 'And not for that reason,' she said when Mandy opened her mouth. 'I didn't have much rest over the weekend.'

'Was your parents' anniversary that good?'

'Yeah,' Autumn said. 'It was touch and go for a moment. Some other time,' she told Mandy with a wave of her hand, 'but they're still in love. It's nauseating.'

'I don't think so,' Mandy said, her expression dreamy. 'I think it's brilliant. Two old people, still in love after all these years.'

'My parents are not old.'

Mandy stared at her.

'They're older,' Autumn conceded, 'and, trust me, it's less appealing when your mother and father are sticking their tongues down each other's throats.'

Mandy pulled a face. 'Ugh.'

'Exactly.' She paused, and when the thought popped in her mind, Autumn went with it. 'Could you keep an eye on things for a few hours?'

'Sure.' Mandy frowned. 'Are you okay?'

'Yeah. I thought I'd try and catch an hour of sleep before I switch the sugar with salt in a batch of cupcakes.'

Mandy winced. 'You don't have to keep bringing that up, you know. I felt bad enough when it happened.'

'Me too, considering I can still taste it.' She mock shuddered, and then laughed when Mandy mimicked throwing something at her. 'Don't worry. I'll only bring it up until you do something similarly atrocious.'

Mandy glowered at her, and Autumn grinned.

See, a voice in her head told her, *you can do this. You*

*can totally pretend like your brain isn't malfunctioning
and your heart isn't questioning your sanity.*

Except she wasn't sure how sustainable it was. It felt as
if she was offering Mandy a fake shiny version of herself
that would crack if anyone stared at it too long.

'I'll see you later,' Autumn said, taking her apron off
and grabbing her purse and keys.

'Don't think you got away from the Hunter question,'
Mandy called after her.

Autumn's shoulders immediately tightened. She didn't
bother turning around, just lifted a hand in a wave and left
Mandy to speculate.

She didn't mind Mandy's curiosity. They weren't simply friends because they worked together. Mandy didn't
ever question who Autumn was, or seem to expect anything from her. Autumn didn't have to worry about being
on, though most of the time, she couldn't help it.

She was always playing a role. Perfect daughter. Perfect sister. Perfect girlfriend. And asking herself questions:
what did her mother, sister, boyfriend need from her? Who
did she need to be to provide it?

The problem with it was that she was consistently putting others first. More significantly, she was placing herself last. Just like with the situation with Hunter, she knew
what moulding herself to other people's needs would bring
her. Disappointment when they didn't see her, appreciate her. Hurt when their actions told her they didn't value
her efforts.

And just like with Hunter, she couldn't figure out why
she still did it.

She gritted her teeth, pausing to catch her breath. Seconds later she realised she'd reached her house. She looked
up at the tall white building with the dark wooden frames.
After years, it still made her happy. Her steps crunched on
the white pebbled pathway, and she tried to let the roses
along it calm her as she made her way to her patio.

It was a simple pleasure, standing there and looking at the city she'd grown up in. Buildings of various colours looked back at her, along with Table Mountain in the far distance, and bodies of water and houses. If she looked to the left, she could see the green grass spilling over the inclines and declines of her property. If she walked in that direction, she'd be able to see the river she could sometimes hear at night.

She took a deep breath and settled down on one of the recliners she'd bought for the pool. Her body sighed in relief. It felt as if it had been in a fight. Or perhaps it felt as if it was preparing for an onslaught. She'd barely got any sleep the night before, the thought of Hunter in the other room too much of a distraction. The memory of what he'd told her too much of a disturbance.

I'm a father.

She wanted to take those words and crumple them up. Throw them down at the city she loved so much. They filled her with so much pain, though she couldn't pinpoint exactly why. Was it because they symbolised something she would never have? Certainly not with him. Or was it because they confirmed that he'd moved on from her?

She had no right to be upset about it. He hadn't cheated on her. They'd broken up. And while she'd stayed on her couch for weeks, crying about a man she'd thought would fulfil the perfect plans she'd had for them, he'd been giving someone else everything she'd wanted.

Autumn.

She sighed, knocked her head lightly against the headrest of the recliner. She couldn't help him if she felt like this. Since she'd already agreed to it, she didn't have much choice now. She would just be…cautious. She would try and protect herself.

Though she wasn't sure how she was going to do it, she was content with realising she had to. Content enough to close her eyes and sleep as the sun's rays touched her legs.

* * *

Grace would be bringing Eli, his son, over in an hour. He paced the room, the thought of it, the realisation of it, worrying him as he waited for Autumn to arrive. He needed her with him so his mind would stop tripping over itself. So his heart wouldn't feel as if it were beating in a compressed space.

He ignored the guilt that accompanied the need.

It had encouraged him to offer to pick her up, though. She'd refused.

'Even if we ignore how silly it would be for you to drive an hour out of the city to help me,' she'd started in a tone that had brooked no disagreement, 'how would you take me home when you have a three-month-old to get settled?'

He hadn't even considered that, which had pushed his thoughts back over a cliff.

He was worried, deeply, that he wouldn't be a good father. That he'd follow his father's footsteps and act selfishly. Or that he wouldn't be able to give his son what he needed.

That fear was deeper than the ones he had about repeating his father's mistakes, though more obscured. He could see it was there, like a red light flickering under black material, but he didn't know what it said. His emotions curling into themselves, rocking back and forth, told him it had to do with Janie. But he couldn't unfurl the emotions or still their movement long enough to figure it out.

So they stayed in his stomach, making him ill. And he waited for Autumn to arrive so he wouldn't have to focus on them.

The doorbell rang then; an answer to his prayers. He nearly flung it open in his haste, and his throat went dry. Every part of him stilled, his eyes sweeping over Autumn.

There was one tiny part that began moving again though, jumping up and down, telling him he couldn't do this. He couldn't be overwhelmed by how beautiful she was. He had to pretend he didn't find her attractive. But he nearly snorted at that part because *he had eyes in his head.* He couldn't pretend the woman standing in front of him didn't take his breath away.

She was wearing a pretty summer dress, peach-coloured, which somehow stood out against and moulded to her bronze-tinted skin. Her hair had been tied back into a bunch of curls at the nape of her neck. He was sure that when she turned around, he'd see a ribbon the same colour as her dress keeping it there.

The dress scooped over her neck, giving him a tantalising glimpse of her cleavage; it ended right above her knee, giving him a generous view of smooth, defined legs. The gold sandals she wore wound around feet he'd always thought extraordinary and clung to ankles he could remember kissing.

Logically, he knew he wouldn't be able to run from the fact that he was attracted to her. Because it was simply that—a fact. And he was an adult, who could process facts and control impulses.

But he wouldn't lie: at that moment, it felt as if the universe were testing his ability to do either.

'I was going to say hello,' Autumn said slowly, 'but considering your expression, I now feel like I should ask about your fire extinguisher?'

A fierce blush hit his face.

'I have wine.'

'Hello to you, too,' she said, amusement making her even more beautiful. Annoyingly so. He nearly growled. 'Wine sounds lovely.'

She walked in, past him, and he let out a tight breath he hadn't realised he'd been holding. After giving himself a stern talking-to, he followed her into the kitchen, and poured her a glass of wine. He didn't pour himself one, though he wanted it. Or something stronger. But he couldn't drink when he had to take care of a kid. Besides, he'd been put off by drinking since it had put him in his current predicament. Abstinence—in more than one way—was his strategy moving forward.

'You've set the table,' she commented, sipping from her wine, looking around.

His eyes moved over to the dining room, which he'd decorated with the white runner his mother had sent him when she'd visited the Seychelles some time back. Since he'd opened the glass sliding doors leading into his garden— things had seemed too stifling otherwise—he'd added two citronella candles on either side of the table. He'd thrown some straw placemats around the table after, thinking it made his place look homely. Now, he wondered.

'Too much?'

'No, it's nice.' She turned to face him, and her expression softened. 'You've got to calm down, Hunter.'

'I'm perfectly calm,' he lied.

Her brow arched. 'Really? So that twitch at your right eye is because you're Zen, huh?'

'Just a tic.'

'The frown, too?'

He immediately relaxed his forehead.

She rolled her eyes. 'Why are you nervous?'

He made a hand gesture that was supposed to indicate everything. She nodded.

'Well, the upside is things can hardly go worse than the first two times you've met her. Neither of them was particular positive, I don't think.'

'Hey,' he said without heat.

'What?' she asked dryly. 'You think you're a stud when you're drunk? Because I've got to tell you—'

'You've never complained.'

'You always made up for it sober.' Her mouth curved up at the side, though the rest of her face was tight. 'She didn't have that opportunity.'

He grunted. Tried to figure out what he felt about the

casual way she was talking about him having sex with another woman. It couldn't be easy for her—or perhaps he was overestimating how much she cared about his love life. Then he remembered how she'd needed him to tell her nothing more was going on between him and Grace. And what her face had looked like as she'd asked.

Maybe not.

Except that she was dealing with this pretty casually, which was messing with his head. Did he have to tiptoe around it? Or could he talk about it freely? Not that he wanted to.

'Just ask me whatever's going on in your head instead of trying to figure it out,' she told him wanly. He took a deep breath, then let it out with a shake of his head.

'Fine, then.' Her grip was tight on the wine glass. 'I'll ask you this. Why does she trust you to take care of the child? She doesn't know you.'

'She doesn't have a choice. She doesn't have any family. She was visiting a friend here when…' He trailed off.

Her eyes narrowed. 'There's more.'

'She thinks I'm decent,' he said, unsurprised by her intuition.

'Based on what?'

'Not sure. You'll have to ask her.'

'What's available on the Internet does make you look good.' She gently swirled the wine in her glass, tilting her head to the side. 'The fact that your company provides renewable energy to townships. The charity work. That video of you—'

'Autumn.'

'I was going to say presenting the cheque to the CF Institute,' she said dryly. 'Also, the donation to the non-profit caring for orphaned CF kids. How you spent the day with them.' The pause before her next words lasted only seconds. 'Though being the Bakery Boyfriend must have been what swayed her.'

She grinned. He wanted to scowl back, but of course he didn't. Instead, he smiled, and wished he could capture the moment to return to later. The little bubble of warmth floating in his chest because of her would no doubt pop soon, and he wanted to protect it for as long as he could.

He'd done the same thing in their relationship, when he'd started realising he couldn't have a future with Autumn. But he'd known then, just as he did now, that he was living on borrowed time. Seconds later, his time ran out.

'You don't have to be afraid,' she told him, settling the glass down. 'You know how to take care of a child.'

'I've never taken care of a baby.' The word came out hoarsely, and he cleared his throat. 'I don't know how to.'

'You'll learn.'

She said it so simply he wanted to believe her.

'How do you know?'

'When you interact with them enough, you're forced to. I'm speaking, of course, as someone who was coerced into taking care of my mother's friends' kids. Clearly, I'm an expert.' Her voice softened. 'Your baby is too small for you to mess up anyway,' she said gently. 'You just have to keep the kid alive.'

'What if I can't?' The words sprang from his tongue; his hands curled into fists. 'What if I can't keep him alive, Autumn? What then?'

CHAPTER FIVE

'WHAT?' AUTUMN ASKED, her voice shaky. 'Why would you think that?'

He took the glass from her hand, brought it to his lips, but set it down again before he could drink it. His knuckles were turning white as he gripped the counter instead, and then he lowered his arms. Deliberately, she thought.

'I didn't mean it,' he said after a long pause. 'But that's why you're here.' He offered her a forced smile. 'So I don't say stupid things like that again.'

'That's what I'm here for?'

'For moral support,' he confirmed.

'And part of providing moral support is making sure you don't say anything as concerning as you just did?'

'It's not concerning. It was…a joke.'

'A joke,' she repeated, staring at him.

He gave a curt nod, and she wondered if he really expected her to believe him. He didn't say anything else, which told her he did.

Hunter's entire demeanour had been concerning since she'd arrived. But this? This was the worst. And she knew it had something to do with his sister. What, how, she wasn't sure, but her gut told her that it did. Her gut was usually right when it came to Hunter.

He'd told her about his sister pretty early on. There hadn't been much detail in the information he'd provided though. Autumn only knew his sister had been sick with cystic fibrosis and had passed away at the age of ten.

Whenever she'd build up the courage to ask about it, he'd clam up and change the subject. Much as he was doing now—and maybe *that* was how she knew this had something to do with Janie.

It would make sense if he was afraid about his son being ill. She'd been snarky about it in her thoughts the day before—and now felt bad for it—but she knew how much carrying the cystic fibrosis gene weighed on him.

Before deciding to end their relationship, they'd had what felt like millions of conversations about it. He'd told her he didn't want children because there'd be a chance they might get sick, however small. He'd refused genetic counselling; he couldn't put them through what he'd been through, he'd told her. He hadn't wanted it—even the possibility of it—to hang over his kid's head as it had his.

'What about adoption?' she'd asked then.

'No.'

Her heart had broken. 'Just like that?'

'No,' he said, softer this time. 'I... I shouldn't have children. I won't be a good father.'

'Why would you say that?'

'It's true.' The look on his face had made her doubt it. 'I don't want to have a family.'

That had been their last conversation before ending things.

'Hunter,' she started, lifting a hand to her aching heart, 'I hope this isn't because you think you'll be a bad father.'

He lifted a shoulder.

'You won't be,' she assured him. She nearly reached out, grasped his hand. Praised herself when she didn't. 'But I can't help keep you from saying something concerning. I'd have to stop you from speaking entirely.'

His lips curved, then he sobered. 'Thank you for being here.'

She was about to say, 'It's a pleasure', but stopped herself. Felt an unreasonable pride for doing so, same as when she'd praised herself—also unreasonably—for not taking his hand.

It was just that... Those were things she would do to try and be perfect. The perfect supporter in this case. But she didn't want to touch him and feel the heat that touching him always brought. And being there for him *wasn't* a pleasure; no, it was torture.

They were small things, but they felt significant somehow. Selfish, but significant.

She left it at that, unable to make sense of it, though silence had fallen on them. The longer it extended, the harder the little men dancing in that space between her heart and stomach danced. The wilder they danced.

'Okay.' She bit her lip. 'Now *I'm* nervous.'

His eyes swept over her face, amusement taking some of the strain away. 'You don't have to be.'

She made a non-committal sound.

'You don't,' he insisted. 'Grace is going to look at you and know...' He trailed off.

'That we have a weird relationship?' she teased through the lump in her throat.

He didn't smile.

'No,' he said after a moment. 'She'll know I have support. She won't worry as much.'

'I doubt that.'

'Your support will help me be a decent parent.'

'That's a lot of pressure to put on a weird relationship,' she said lightly, though the lump was growing.

His eyes lifted to hers. 'Maybe. But I don't think she'll deny that you make me a better person.'

Her fingers tightened on the stem of her glass; her head went light. No, it was her heart. Filling with helium, floating up into her head, screwing with her thoughts. She forced herself to think of all the reasons why she couldn't allow herself to fall for his charm.

He had a child. There was no future for them. He didn't want a future with *her*.

It worked. Remembering all of it popped her heart, caused the broken, deflated pieces to fall back into her chest. Very deliberately, she brought the glass to her lips, took a deep sip.

'I know this isn't an ideal situation for either of us,' he said quietly. 'Least of all for you. I…appreciate you.'

She nodded. Searched her mind desperately for something to change the subject with.

'Did you warn her I'd be here?'

'Yes,' Hunter said. 'I told her I'd have a close friend with me.'

'Did you tell her it was me?' she asked. 'No, wait—did you say it like that?'

'No and yes.' He paused. 'I'm not sure what the second refers to.'

'Did you call me a "close" friend?'

She lifted her hands in air quotes, and lowered them both to her glass.

'You don't think we're close?'

'It's not about that. It's about you describing your ex-girlfriend as a close friend to the mother of your child.'

He shrugged. 'It's true.'

Warmth sank into her bones. A desperate, inappropriate warmth that had no business being in her body at all.

'Ten more minutes,' she said, for lack of anything else.

'Yeah.'

It was all either of them said for the longest time. Her mind teased her, told her to talk, though it provided nothing good to say. Only illogical things. Things unsuitable to the tension of the anticipation of the baby and his mother's arrival.

As if to taunt her further, it offered her the memory of how Hunter had looked at her when she'd arrived. Up to this moment, she'd been able to ignore it. Or not ignore it, since that seemed impossible, but to manage it.

She hadn't burst into flames when she'd met Hunter's eyes and seen the fire there. In fact, she'd *joked*. She'd pretended not to see how good he looked in his shirt and jeans. Hadn't commented on his smell when she'd forgotten to stop inhaling as she'd passed him. Automatically, unexpectedly, it had made her knees go weak. It smelled like nothing else in the world. It smelled like *Hunter*.

Her face started to warm, and, heaven help her, so did other parts of her body. She wanted to reach for her glass of wine, but it was empty. Considering Grace would be there any minute, she'd need her wits about her. Autumn couldn't pour herself another glass, regardless of how strong the temptation was.

She'd have to resist it just as she had to resist her attraction to him. She would put it aside. She'd done it with her emotional feelings for him; she could do it with her physical feelings, too. So she'd focus on...how annoyingly grumpy he was instead.

In defiance, her mind reminded her how attracted she was to that grumpiness. A combination of reticence and shyness struggling with the assertiveness he needed as a CEO of a company worth billions. The grumpiness made her want to strangle him and coddle him and—

She almost threw her hands up in frustration. Maybe she should jump him and get it over with. Maybe that would finally sate the heat. But she knew there was no sating this...this *need*. She'd spent two satisfactory years proving that.

'Are you okay?' Hunter asked, his eyes on her face.

It burned, and she turned, embarrassed. Logically, she knew he couldn't see into her head. He couldn't know she was thinking about pulling him into the bedroom when the mother of his child—*and his child*—were minutes away.

'Autumn?'

'I'm fine,' she said brightly, turning back. 'Sorry.' She pressed her hands to her cheeks. 'I think I drank the wine too quickly.'

He studied her, his lips parting as if he wanted to say

something, but the bell rang and distracted him. *Thank you*, she told the universe, even as her stomach rolled with nerves. She nodded at him, and he went to open the door as she smoothed down the front of her dress.

Seconds later, she grabbed the wine bottle and her wine glass and put them on the counter behind a wall separating part of the kitchen from the rest of it. She didn't want Grace to see she'd been drinking. The last thing she wanted was for Grace to realise how comfortable she was at Hunter's place. It would create an insider versus outsider impression Autumn wanted to avoid.

Although, to be honest, Autumn wasn't entirely sure which side she fell on.

Taking a deep breath, she rested a hand on her stomach as though somehow it would help still the dancing men there. It didn't. In fact, it didn't even encourage the air she'd breathed in to move to where the fluttering was.

She closed her eyes, cursed silently. Then she straightened her shoulders and moved back to the main part of the kitchen.

Hunter and Grace were already in the living room, front door closed. On the floor was a car seat that had, for the moment, no sound coming from it. Embarrassed that she'd taken so long to steady herself, she moved forward, her eyes stuck on Grace.

She was beautiful. Shorter than Autumn, her hair in a long, straight ponytail that fell to the middle of her back. Her features were dark; though they were tight now. Unhappy. When Grace saw Autumn, her spine straightened. Autumn understood. She wasn't feeling particularly at ease herself.

'Hi,' Autumn said, moving forward and offering a hand. 'I'm Autumn Bishop.'

'Grace Tatum,' the woman said, taking Autumn's hand. The grip was hot, a little sweaty, and Grace grimaced.

Autumn shook her head slightly, as if to say, *Never mind.* Grace's face eased somewhat.

'It's nice to meet you,' Grace continued, before dropping her hand. 'I'm sorry…these are the circumstances.'

'Oh,' Autumn said with a frown. 'You don't have to be.'

Grace's eyes slipped to Hunter's, then back to Autumn. 'You're not upset?'

'About what?'

Grace's brow knitted. 'Did Hunter tell you why I'm here? Or who I am?'

'Of course I did.' Hunter spoke for the first time. 'I wouldn't have asked her to join me if I hadn't been honest.'

Autumn sent Hunter a look, hoping it conveyed her message: *Calm down.* Grace wasn't questioning his integrity, which was what Hunter's defensive reaction implied. She was…curious. Uncertain. Hunter angled his head, as if understanding. She almost sighed out loud.

This is why you shouldn't have called me a close friend.

'I know who you are, Grace,' Autumn said. 'But I think you're under the wrong impression about who I am.' Her mouth curved, even as her stomach tightened in anxiety. 'Hunter and I are friends. *Only* friends.'

All the muscles in Hunter's body tightened. 'I told you that,' he said again.

Autumn gave him another look, but a strong desire for Grace to know he hadn't been lying about his and Autumn's relationship spurred his words. For reasons he'd rather not question, he wanted Autumn to know, too.

'I know,' Grace said softly. 'But I didn't know whether I should believe you. People aren't always honest about these things.'

'I am,' Hunter said firmly.

Autumn shook her head, as if she'd given up on him. 'It's true,' she said, 'he is. He's also a tad defensive, as you can tell.'

Grace smiled, her grip on the straps of the handbag she wore across her body tightening, then loosening.

'We're really only friends though,' Autumn said again. Again, Hunter felt something loop in his stomach. Why did her insistence about the nature of their relationship bother him so much? 'And if you're not comfortable with me being here, I'll leave.'

Hunter fought to keep the panic he felt from appearing on his face. Or taking a hold of his tongue. His expression remained blanked, hopefully. He kept quiet.

'Oh, no, that's not necessary,' Grace said. 'I…wish I had support.' Her eyes lowered to the car seat. Hunter hadn't been able to look down yet.

'You don't have anyone?' Autumn asked.

'None who were willing to help me with this,' Grace said with a faint smile. 'Hell of a thing to figure out when visiting those people got me into this situation.'

There was an awkward pause.

'You don't have any family?' Autumn asked softly.

Grace's face tightened. She stood a little taller. 'My parents died when I was younger. I have no siblings, and no extended family that would help.' Her eyes met Autumn's. 'Satisfied?'

'Of course,' Autumn said with a shake of her head. 'I didn't mean to imply… I'm sorry.'

Grace deflated. 'No,' she said after a beat. 'I'm sorry. I shouldn't have reacted like that.' She took a breath. 'It's just that… This has been harder than I expected. I thought I could—' She broke off. Another beat passed before she straightened her shoulders. 'I was starting my second year of articles when I found out I was pregnant. I worked for as long as I could, and I got maternity leave, but it's unpaid, and my savings have run out.'

'I can help,' Hunter said. His voice sounded harsh in his ears.

'No, thank you,' Grace said primly. 'It would only be a

temporary fix anyway. I have to finish my articles before I can start working, and I've had an offer at a law firm here.' Her hands tightened on the strap of her bag again. 'If I want to provide for Eli—and I do—I need to do this. The sooner, the better.' She hesitated. 'I want to do it now, before he grows up to realise being irresponsible got me here. I'm trying to counteract the irresponsible with the responsible.' Grace looked at him and winced. 'Sorry.'

He shrugged. He agreed with her assessment.

'Look, I know what you're thinking. What kind of mother would—'

'We're not,' Autumn interrupted.

Grace's expression softened. 'Thank you.' She ran a hand down her ponytail, before bringing the hair to rest over her shoulder. 'I want my son to believe I did everything I could to give him a good life. If it means being away from him for three months, then so be it. I'll do whatever I have to to give him his best life.'

'And you trust me to take care of him?' Hunter asked, unable to resist.

It had been a question that had plagued him since even before Autumn had brought it up. Since Grace had asked him to take care of Eli, in fact. He'd seen Janie's face in Eli's, and his mind had been inundated with memories and emotions. The question—though not the reasons for it—had been the only clear thing.

'In all honesty?' Grace asked. 'Yes. I know how that makes me look. But...but if I want to teach Eli to judge people fairly, then I can't mummy-shame mothers. Even if that mother is me.' She paused. 'My instincts tell me I can trust you. I've done a fair amount of research about you—I've watched videos and seen pictures—and you seem like a decent person. So do you,' Grace added, addressing Autumn. Autumn simply nodded.

Grace turned her attention back to Hunter.

'The little I can remember about our night together

makes me think it's okay to trust you. Besides, he's your son, too, and you know me just as well as I know you. If I want you to trust me, I figure that has to go both ways.'

'Then there's something you should know,' Hunter forced himself to say. He felt Autumn shift closer to him. It helped him speak, despite the swelling that suddenly seemed to surround his vocal cords. 'There's a chance Eli might be sick.'

Grace's expression went blank.

CHAPTER SIX

THE MEN IN Autumn's stomach were still there. Their dancing had turned into something less wild now, more choreographed, their steps hammering in sync against her chest bone at the tension in the room. She took another step closer to Hunter.

'I'm a carrier of the cystic fibrosis gene.' Hunter's voice sounded detached. Autumn supposed it was the only way he could get himself through it. 'My… My sister had the disease.'

'Had?'

Autumn felt the muscles in Hunter's body coil. 'She passed away.'

'What?' Grace's face was stricken. 'Are you telling me my son could *die*?'

'No,' Autumn answered when Hunter didn't say anything. 'No,' she said again for good measure. 'Hunter's only a carrier of the gene.'

'What the hell does that mean?'

'For Eli to be sick,' Autumn continued after a quick glance at Hunter's face told her he wouldn't be replying, 'you have to be a carrier, too. Are you?'

'Of cystic fibrosis?' Grace shook her head. 'I don't know. My parents weren't sick. I… I don't know if there are other family members who have it.' She sucked in her lip. 'I should ask. I should—'

'Grace,' Autumn interrupted the spiral. 'You know that you're not sick, right?' she asked. Grace nodded. 'So even if you are a carrier, Eli only has a twenty-five per cent chance of having this disease.'

'But…but what if he *is* sick?' Grace's eyes widened; her voice dropped. 'What if I didn't notice?'

'This isn't your fault,' Autumn said firmly. She took a breath. 'It's not either of your faults.' She waited a beat. 'It might not even be something we have to worry about. We should make sure of that first.'

'How?' Grace asked.

It seemed that Hunter had lost his voice. Autumn almost sighed.

'Babies aren't automatically tested for CF here when they're born, but we can request a test. We'll do that as soon as possible. We'll make an appointment.'

'My flight to Johannesburg is in three hours,' Grace whispered. 'I don't have the money to change it. I start work *tomorrow morning*,' she added more urgently.

Autumn glanced over at Hunter again, but he was still staring straight ahead, as if to escape the conversation.

'We can do this without you.' Autumn deliberately softened her voice. 'We'll keep in touch every step of the way. Trust, right?' she said, when Grace didn't reply.

Grace nodded slowly. 'Okay.' Her chest heaved. 'I can't do everything by myself.' That part was muttered. 'This is what we have to do. Co-parent. Share the responsibilities. Yeah?'

She gave a brave smile. When Hunter didn't say anything, Autumn nudged him. He blinked, rapidly, his gaze meeting Grace's.

'Of course.' He cleared his throat. 'We'll figure this out.'

'Okay.' Her gaze lowered to the car seat, then up to Hunter. 'Would you like to meet your son?'

Hunter nodded.

He'd watched a sci-fi movie once, where the lead character had been sucked into a different dimension. She walked and walked, but the dimension was nothingness. She refused to give up. She walked until her feet bled. Until she was dying of exertion and dehydration; still, she walked. And eventually, when she felt she couldn't go on, she found a door that had led home.

Seeing Eli for the first time was strangely like that.

Hunter felt as if he were in a different dimension. The insides of his body felt as though they were inflating, growing and growing, and soon his skin wouldn't be able to contain them. The air in his lungs seemed like too much, and perhaps that was what was causing his insides to inflate.

But Hunter kept looking at the little boy in Grace's arms.

Everything he'd been worried about faded to the background. Back to earth, he thought distractedly, while he was walking in this different dimension. As he took in Eli's features—the dark mass of hair, the small, puckered mouth—and saw his sister in them, he knew nothing would ever matter as much as this.

He'd felt the same way about Janie, he thought, blinking, mortified that tears heated his eyes.

Despite the overwhelming swell of emotion, he knew he would walk and walk and walk until his feet bled and he was dying if it meant walking to Eli. Thinking about everything he'd been through in his life, perhaps he already had.

'Hi,' Grace said softly. She shifted Eli in her arms so that he was facing Hunter. So that he was watching Hunter with the brown eyes that came from his family. 'Say hi to your dad, Eli.'

The baby didn't make a sound, just kept watching Hunter. Hunter couldn't resist his smile. The kid was already like him, realising talking wasn't as important as observing. Warmth sparked in his chest.

'Do you want to hold him?'

Hunter automatically took a step back before he felt a hand on his shoulder. He looked to his side, saw Autumn standing there. The hesitancy melted away.

'Yes. Please,' he said. 'How do I…?'

'Just support his neck like this.'

Grace showed him, speaking in soothing tones, though he didn't know whether that was for his benefit or Eli's. She seemed to have recovered from her earlier shock, or maybe he was witnessing her resilience when it came to parenting their son. Sensing the latter was true, Hunter's respect for her grew.

He thought no more of it when his son was successfully transferred to his arms.

Eli was so small. That was Hunter's first thought. He felt like a lumbering giant holding the little guy. He was sure he looked it, too. But it didn't matter that much to him. As long as Eli was safe and comfortable, Hunter didn't care whether he looked like a novice or a fool.

His second thought was that Eli was perfect. He didn't count Eli's fingers or toes; didn't know if he was sick or not. But he was perfect. And for the rest of his life, Hunter would make sure his son knew it.

His third thought…

He'd already turned to Autumn before he'd fully realised it. He lowered his forearm, where Eli's body was resting, showing him to Autumn.

'Did you see him?'

Her cheeks lifted in a small smile. 'I did. I do.'

'He's perfect.'

The smile widened. 'He is.'

'Do you want to hold him?' He turned to Grace, belatedly realising he shouldn't simply make those kinds of decisions. 'Can she?'

'Of course,' Grace said, lifting a hand.

Hunter looked back at Autumn. 'Do you?'

Autumn's eyes flicked from Grace to him. She pursed her lips, then relaxed them, and smiled at him again. 'I'd love to.'

He handed Eli over to her, imitating what Grace had done. Autumn accepted Eli easily, shifting as soon as she had a hold on him to get one more comfortably. Hunter stepped back, watching. Smiling. She already looked a million times more comfortable than he had, he was sure. She moved gently, back and forth, lifting a hand and taking Eli's hand with her thumb and index finger.

'It's very nice to meet you, Eli,' she said softly, still moving. 'My name is Autumn. I'm your dad's friend.' She shook Eli's hand. Hunter's heart swelled. 'I suppose that makes me your aunt. Not a real one,' she clarified, 'one of those weird ones who call themselves aunts but have no real relation.'

She looked at Grace. 'He's beautiful. Congratulations.'

Graced smiled. For the first time, it was completely genuine. 'Thank you.'

'You, too, Daddy,' Autumn said, looking at him now, too. 'Good work.'

Hunter didn't know how to feel. He supposed meeting Eli had something to do with it. He was overwhelmed. Emotions he hadn't felt in years had exploded inside him. A fierce protectiveness. A willingness to sacrifice anything to make Eli's life easier. He hadn't felt either of those things since Janie's death. Remembering them had a peculiar effect on his heart.

Except...

That wasn't entirely true, and perhaps that was what had put him off. He'd felt those same feelings with Autumn. They were somehow different at the same time, but just as fierce. And as terrifying.

It took seeing her hold his son to realise he'd been scared when he'd realised what she wanted from their relationship. They were completely normal things to want: spending a life together, having a family. Hell, *he* wanted them—with her. But he hadn't been able to risk it. Because risking it meant the possibility of...of losing it, too.

He wouldn't be able to handle that. Not again.

'Can I explain his schedule to you?' Grace asked.

Hunter blinked. Slowly nodded.

'I've written it all down, but basically…'

She told him about Eli's feeding and sleep schedule, explaining it with the book she'd written it down in. Hunter listened attentively, relieved to have something other than his thoughts to focus on.

'You can call me any time of the day or night,' Grace said at the end of it. 'I'll answer when I can, and get in touch as soon as possible after if I can't.'

'Okay.'

'If you need anything—'

'I'll call,' Hunter told her. 'I'll have my lawyer get in touch about child support. We can discuss custody once you're settled back here.'

Grace stared at him. 'I don't—'

'Let me know if anything concerns you,' Hunter said, as if Grace hadn't interrupted. 'Now, do you have a way to get to the airport?'

She was exhausted. More than ever before. Grace had left shortly after she and Hunter had discussed Eli's schedule. Autumn had suggested she and Hunter give Grace a private moment to say goodbye, and things had been disturbingly tense as they'd waited outside on the patio. After Grace had left, Autumn had watched Hunter try to feed Eli.

Eli had started crying almost immediately after his mother had closed the door. Hunter had given Autumn a panicked look, and, calmly, she reminded Hunter of Grace's parting instructions—a bottle, then sleep. She made the bottle while Hunter tried to calm Eli, but his efforts were futile. The baby only cried louder, in those ragged, hoarse sobs only babies possessed.

She silently asked the universe why it had done this. Hunter needed a baby that barely cried; one that wouldn't scare him away from parenting his kid. But the universe refused to take responsibility, gesturing wildly in her personified state at the awkward way Hunter was holding his son. He was clearly uncomfortable with Eli, the ease he'd shown when he'd first held the boy disappearing now that Grace was gone.

She finished the bottle quickly, then offered it to Hunter. He shook his head, taking it from her hand and setting it on the table before handing Eli to her. She accepted without a complaint, though her insides wanted her to. Loudly. Vehemently. Just as the emotions she was still processing demanded.

Because they made her feel as though she'd been ploughed over by an avalanche, she didn't. She could only imagine what he was going through. So she'd give him the benefit of the doubt for now.

And ignore your own feelings in the process.

She did exactly that. Though her heart begged her to take heed of the carnage this experience had left in its wake, she fed Eli. Burped him. Put him to sleep. She ignored Hunter's piercing gaze as he watched it all—to judge himself with later, she knew. When she finally set down Eli in the brand-new crib she found in Hunter's spare room, her body was aching from the strain.

'Are you okay?' he asked eventually.

'I should be asking you that,' she said, as her heart screamed.

'This was…intense.'

'Yes.'

'So you're not okay.'

She didn't answer. The silence stretched.

'I'm sorry,' he said.

She shook her head. 'Don't… You have nothing to apologise for.'

'I couldn't even feed my son.'

'You didn't try,' she said sharply. Released a breath. 'Hold on. I need a moment.'

He gave it to her.

She closed her eyes. Struggled to gain control of her emotions. The truth was, she wished she hadn't agreed to be there that evening. What she'd witnessed had twisted her gut. It had been touching and beautiful. It had obviously impacted Hunter.

It had taken all of her strength not to sink down to the floor and sob.

Seeing Hunter—*her* Hunter—holding a baby, looking at the child as if he were the most important thing in Hunter's life had broken her. Because she couldn't help but think of how it would have been to see Hunter look at *their* child like that. If only he'd been open to taking a chance with her.

She opened her eyes again when she heard Hunter closing the windows and doors. He joined her on the couch when he saw her watching him, sitting at the opposite end. They spent another while in silence.

'You're going to have to try,' she said eventually. 'Even when things are hard.'

'I know.'

'That's not enough. You have to do, too.'

'I know.'

The anger in his tone put her back up.

'No,' she said. Whatever had been holding her back before had disappeared. '*You* asked for help. How is it fair that you're angry at me simply because you don't like what I have to say?'

'I'm not angry at you,' he snapped.

'Really? You seem pretty angry.'

'I am, but not at you. Or about what you've said.' He paused. 'I'm angry at myself.'

'Why?'

'Because I'm acting exactly like my father did.'

CHAPTER SEVEN

'TELL ME.'

It was a simple question; he heard it as a command. He wasn't sure what authority Autumn had over him. Didn't know why he felt he needed to obey her. Still, he did.

'He didn't help to take care of Janie,' he said. He didn't want to tiptoe around it any longer. But it felt strange speaking plainly. 'When she was sick.'

'Okay,' Autumn said after a moment. 'What does that have to do with the way you're treating Eli now?'

'I'm… I'm not taking care of him.' Couldn't she see it? 'I'm not doing what I should be doing.'

'You say that as if you don't have a choice in the matter.'

His reply died on his lips before he could utter it. It took a long time for him to ask, 'But what if I don't do it right?'

'Do you think Janie would have cared whether your father did it *right*?' she asked. 'Or would it have been more important to her that he tried?'

He had no reply for that, so he nodded, accepting the slight accusation in her tone. He had those accusations, too, of himself. Could see that he was conveniently leaning in to the excuse of his father for the moment. Wasn't sure how he knew it—or why he saw it so clearly—but he was excusing his behaviour when he shouldn't be.

A part of him continued to do it. It reminded him of how the meeting had been harder than he'd expected. Telling Grace that their child might be sick had been harder than expected. Hearing the utter terror in her voice had transported him back to each doctor's appointment he'd accompanied his mother to.

He'd been much too young to accompany her and listen to such news, he'd realised later. He'd also realised that she'd needed the support, even if it had come from her barely eleven—then thirteen, then sixteen-year-old son. Because even at that age Hunter had heard the fear in his mother's voice as she'd asked the doctor questions about Janie's condition. He'd go stand beside her, take her hand and squeeze. Then he'd go back to Janie and try to distract her.

The memories had paralysed him. When Grace had left and Eli had started crying, there had been a moment when he'd wanted to run away. He'd seen his father in that, and had, for the first time, sympathised with the man. Had Calvin Lee been terrified, too? Had he felt too overwhelmed to do anything about his child's needs?

It was a complicated thing to empathise with his father. On the one hand, he could understand his father's actions. On the other, they'd contributed to his. The memories that had Hunter feeling terrified and overwhelmed might not have been a factor had his father stepped up. It had spurred him to step up, long enough to try to comfort Eli.

But it hadn't worked. Holding Eli's shaking body in his arms had crushed something inside him. He'd desperately grasped at his father's behaviour as a crutch then.

He no longer could now. Because of Autumn.

He was in this situation because of Autumn.

'None of this would have happened if we hadn't broken up,' he said quietly, anger pulsing in his body, in his veins.

'You're…you're blaming this on our break-up?'

His sanity intervened, keeping him from replying.

'You can't blame me for your actions.'

'What about *your* actions?' he demanded.

Apparently, his sanity had fled to greener pastures.

'What?'

'You suspected I didn't want to have a family long before you brought it up, didn't you?'

'What does that have to do with this?'

'We shouldn't have stayed together as long as we did.'

Her eyes widened. The bright lights in his living room

allowed him to see every emotion in them. Guilt pierced his body; he plastered the holes closed with anger.

'Why did you stay, Autumn? If we'd ended things sooner, I wouldn't have been as broken. I wouldn't have fallen as deep and—'

'You're saying it's my fault for not walking away sooner?' Her voice was small, but firm.

'I... I wouldn't have done this if—'

'No,' she said in the same tone. She stood, too, and gave him a look that had every guilty hole in his body open and bleeding. 'I won't let you malign a relationship I, for some silly reason, still hold cherished memories of. I'm going to leave.'

Panic opened his mouth before sanity could.

'What about Eli?'

'He has his more than capable father to take care of him.'

'I *can't.*'

'You have an entire book with instructions.' She paused. Continued more quietly. 'I'm not going to stay here when you're emotional and overwhelmed and lashing out at me because you don't know how to deal with it.'

He was embarrassed at his words, his anger, now that the emotion had passed. Added to it was how embarrassed he was that she knew him so well.

She stood, grabbing her handbag. As she put it on her shoulder, she studied him.

'You're going to be fine.'

He didn't reply.

'You're going to be okay,' Autumn said again, walking to the door. 'I know it doesn't seem like that right now, but you will be.'

She met his eyes, her brown eyes blazing with emotion that had his heart quickening.

'She's lovely, by the way. Grace. So is your son.' She turned, opened the door. 'You have a beautiful family,' she called over her shoulder.

Then she was gone.

He stood before he realised it; paused when he did. He wanted to go after her. Felt compelled to, if he was being honest, though he didn't know what he'd say to her. Trusting that instinct, he walked to the door, then belatedly turned and grabbed the baby monitor. The guilt was somewhat tamed when he saw Eli sleeping soundly. His grip tightened on the device as he opened the door. When he got to the driveway, he stopped.

Since it was evening, the outdoor lighting had already gone on automatically. It gave him the perfect view of Autumn, sitting in her car, her hands braced at ten and twelve on the steering wheel. From where he stood, he could see the white of her knuckles. Her head was hanging, so it took her wiping at her nose with the back of her wrist for him to realise she was crying.

He walked forward slowly, as if approaching a wounded animal. Her head shot up, making him pause as if *he* were the animal, caught in the headlights. But that terrible expression on her face made him think he'd been right in his initial assessment.

She was the wounded one.

He'd wounded her.

Tears fell steadily from her eyes, though they stared unblinkingly at him. Her face showed none of the quiet capability she'd displayed when she'd told him she was leaving. Whatever was there was raw and painful. He felt it as if it were his own emotion.

He moved without truly noticing it. Soon he was opening her car door, placing the monitor on the passenger seat. He reached under her seat then, adjusted it back, and unclicked her seat belt. Bracing a knee on the frame of the door, he pulled her into his arms, getting their bodies as comfortable as he could.

She was stiff at first, and he worried that he might have crossed a boundary. The thought had barely gone through his head before her arms circled his neck and a ragged breath—a sob—escaped from her lips.

And then the words, 'Why wasn't I enough for you, Hunter?'

His arms tightened around her. He could do nothing else as her body shook against his. Each shake sent a stake through his heart. Each stake convinced him he'd been selfish to put her through this. Blaming her for his actions? For his love for her? For his broken heart after their break-up?

He should be blaming himself for staying. For realising as he'd fallen for her that he couldn't give her what she wanted. For ignoring his own experiences for so long that it had taken falling in love and wanting a future to make him realise he couldn't risk having it. Losing it.

He didn't see how a romantic relationship with her would end differently. But a friendship? He wouldn't lose her if she was his friend. He'd been sure of that a week after their break-up. After his one-night stand. He'd felt as if he'd reached some kind of rock bottom then. He'd been under the water again; Autumn, his only way to the surface.

Because of it, he hadn't been surprised when he'd found himself driving to the bakery under the guise of ordering cupcakes for a colleague's birthday.

She'd called him out immediately.

'Really?' she asked dryly. 'There isn't any other place in the actual city of Cape Town for you to get cupcakes from? You had to drive almost an hour to get them from your ex-girlfriend's bakery?'

He winced. It had been the first time he'd realised she was his *ex*-girlfriend.

'They're for Ted,' he replied after a moment. 'He won't accept cupcakes from anyone else.'

She narrowed her eyes. 'You're playing dirty.' She sighed. 'Of course I'll make Ted's birthday cupcakes. It's in two weeks, right?'

'Right.'

There was a beat. 'You know you could have just called this order in.'

'I know.'

Her expression softened. 'I'm glad you didn't. It's nice to see you're still in one piece.'

He'd stayed for a cup of coffee, invited her to a movie that weekend. By the time he'd picked up the cupcakes, their relationship had turned into something new. They'd called it friendship, but it hadn't felt as simple as friendship. It had felt deeper, considering all they'd shared. Though neither of them would ever admit it. At least, they wouldn't have before now.

He shifted when she leaned back. She avoided his gaze as she reached into her handbag, pulling out tissues and dealing with the remnants of the tears. When she finally looked at him, there was no wetness on her face.

But her face was red, podgy; her eyes swollen, as were her nose and lips. It quickened his breath. Made him wonder at her beauty, even in that moment.

'I'm sorry,' she said.

'You don't have to apologise.' He shifted, so he could see her better. 'I should be the one saying sorry.'

'No, I—'

'Why don't you think you were enough for me?' he interrupted.

Her face turned a deeper shade of red and she sniffled. 'Do you really blame me for Eli?'

'No,' he said. 'That wasn't fair.'

'Feelings aren't fair.'

'Good point.' He tried to gather his thoughts. 'There's a part of me that feels that way. But I know it's illogical.'

'It is,' she said quietly. She met his gaze, her face flushing again. 'I tried. I asked about genetic testing. I suggested adoption. I… I tried to make this work.'

'I couldn't give you what you wanted.'

'*You* have it now though.'

Her logic was sound. 'The problem wasn't with you.'

'Hard to believe that considering the current situation.' She looked down at her hands.

He released a shaky breath. 'The current situation is… This is because of my actions. I was wrong to blame you. It was my mistake. Fully.'

Her fingers traced the lines on her palms. He watched the movement. Willed it to hypnotise him. Perhaps then he'd forget she hadn't replied. She hadn't accepted his apology either. The only thing he thought could make it right was to absolve her of the responsibility.

'You don't have to go through this with me. I'm sorry I asked for help.'

She lifted a shoulder. 'We're friends.' Her voice cracked.

'No.' He lifted a hand, cupped her cheek. 'We pretend to be friends. For the sake of the people around us. For the sake of ourselves, too.' His thumb brushed across her skin. 'But we're not friends, Autumn.'

'Okay,' she whispered raggedly. 'What do you call this?'

He laughed, though not out of humour. 'I don't know.' He sobered. 'I honestly don't know.'

Seconds passed.

'Maybe it's better if I'm not a part of this,' she said.

His hand dropped, but she caught it, pulling it into her lap. Her thumbs traced the lines of his palm now.

'Look what it's done to this friendship—or whatever this is—already.'

Pressure built in his chest.

'I felt so stupid in there today,' she continued, 'talking about what *we* were going to do when I have no part in this.'

'You do,' he said, compelled by only heaven knew what. 'You're my…my person.'

Amusement touched her face. 'Is that what I am?'

His lips curved. 'Unless you have another description.'

She leaned back against the seat, her gaze not leaving

his face. 'I don't.' She let out a shaky breath. 'We should have left it at exes.'

His heart ached. 'Okay.'

'It would have been easier.'

'I know.'

'I mean, you'd still be in this situation,' she continued. 'But I would be traipsing in the fields of my estate, thinking about the good old days when you and I were together.'

'You're right,' he said a beat later. 'You don't have to do this.'

She gave him a shrewd look. 'Obviously I wouldn't be traipsing in any field. I'd be missing my person.' Her mouth offered him a half-smile. 'Like it or not, that's what you are.'

'I like it,' he said quietly. He pulled his hand from her grip, taking one of hers in return and bringing it to his lips. 'I'm lucky to have you.'

She lifted her free hand, brushed it over his hair before letting it rest on his shoulder. 'You are.'

He smiled, and it was a long while before he reached for the baby monitor and pulled back. He pressed a kiss to her forehead, standing clear of the car.

'You're free to pull out of this whenever you want to. Whenever you need to,' he added.

She nodded, adjusted her seat and clicked her seat belt back into place. She started the car.

'Thank you.'

'Thank *you*.'

He slammed the door closed and watched as she drove away. When his feet eventually moved, they took him back to the house. Back to his responsibilities.

His guilt followed him.

CHAPTER EIGHT

AUTUMN HATED THAT Hunter had seen her cry. She should have waited until she was at home to let go of her control. At the very least, she should have waited until she was *driving* home. But no, she'd cried in his driveway. Naturally, he'd caught her. And she'd allowed him to comfort her. Confessed her private feelings of inadequacy to him.

Lovely.

She wished she were stronger when it came to him. Or anyone she loved, she realised when she thought of it. Suddenly, doing what he wanted or expected—what her sister, mother, or father wanted or expected—felt like weakness. Which was why she was considering his offer.

You're free to pull out of this whenever you want to. Whenever you need to.

She suspected she needed to. For her own mental health. To move on without him, too. It was time.

That Saturday, she was still trying to come to terms with it. Or force herself into actually doing it. But a five-year-old girl made sure Autumn didn't have time to dwell on it.

A screech brought her to the bakery kitchen. At first, the only thing Autumn could see was the box of the three-tiered cake lying on the floor. Moments later, a woman rushed through the kitchen doors behind Autumn, gasping when she saw the cake. In quick movements, she pulled a small blonde-haired girl to her side, making Autumn notice her for the first time. Her brain filled in the rest.

'Autumn,' Mandy said, dragging her eyes from the floor to Autumn. 'I turned my back for a second. I needed—' She broke off with a moan.

Autumn turned to the mother.

'I thought she was in the bathroom.' The woman's fingers dug into her daughter's shoulders, pulling the girl back against her. 'She's only five.'

Autumn was tempted to ask the mother how old *she* was since she was responsible for the girl. And really, how did she *think* her daughter was in the bathroom?

She gave herself a moment to suppress the thoughts, then to figure out what the hell she was going to do. Exhaling shakily, she met the mother's eyes.

'It's okay. You can finish your meal.'

Visibly relieved, the woman nodded. 'Thank you so much.' Before she left the kitchen, she said, 'I am sorry.'

Autumn nodded, not bothering to reply verbally when she wasn't sure what she'd say. She waited a few seconds after the woman left, then looked at Mandy.

'We have to check the damage.'

'Do we?' Mandy asked in a thin, hopeful voice.

Autumn gave her an indulgent smile, despite the nerves pulsing in her stomach. She squatted so she could straighten the box, Mandy immediately lowering to help. A shifting sound came from inside that had them exchanging a worried look. Together, they set the box on the counter. In careful, quiet movements, they unwrapped the cake.

The tiers had separated, which Autumn had expected considering the impact. But the cake had fallen on its decorated side, destroying the perfect arrangement of flowers they'd toiled over. Some of the fondant had been spoiled, too, particularly between the tiers, but, all things considered, the damage was minimal. It would have been a lot worse if the cake hadn't been packed.

Autumn released a breath. 'Okay, this isn't the end of the world. We'll just reassemble the tiers, fix up the moulds between them. We can check to see if we have some other flowers—' She broke off. 'Why are you looking at me like that?'

'Because you said "we".'

'Yes. You and me.'

'It's my niece's first birthday, remember?' Mandy winced apologetically. 'I'm taking those cupcakes—' she pointed to another box on the counter '—and I have to help set up. But I can call and tell them—'

'No, you go. That isn't something you should miss. Now?' she asked. Mandy nodded. 'Okay, you'll leave now. But I can do this by myself.' That was for her benefit as much as Mandy's. 'Besides, everyone else is here. Wait staff, kitchen staff. Everything will be fine.'

As she said it, one of her waiters burst into the kitchen.

'One of my tables is asking for a manager. His eggs were too soft, and then, not soft enough.'

Autumn opened her mouth, but Mandy waved a hand. 'I'll take care of it.'

Mandy and the waiter left, and Autumn tried to figure out her plan. When panic threatened, she told herself she could do this. This part of her work was the one sphere where she *had* done it. Repeatedly. Successfully. The uncertainty that was her constant companion in life shrank back in the kitchen, though there were moments, like now, where it beat at the doors.

She would not let it in.

The damage could have been worse, she thought again. The entire cake could have been smashed and lying in pieces on the floor. This she could fix, though she had only three hours to do so before delivery. It wouldn't look exactly like the one her client, an old school friend who'd insisted Taste of Autumn make her wedding cake, had ordered, but it wouldn't be terrible.

She wanted to call and warn Mel about the latest development, but she knew she couldn't. She didn't want Mel to worry on her wedding day, especially since there'd still be a Taste of Autumn cake there. But she would deliver the thing herself, explain the situation, and make some kind of restitution. Pleased with the plan, she got to work. She'd just started making the icing when Mandy opened the door.

'Leaving?'

'Yeah.' Mandy's face contorted. 'Are you sure you don't want me to stay and help? I can be late—'

'No,' Autumn interrupted, sifting icing sugar into the butter she had creamed. 'You will not be late. Everything will be fine.'

'Okay, but I'm glad Hunter's here.' Mandy's voice dropped. 'Though he looks a bit the worse for wear. And he has a *baby*.'

Autumn whipped around, spreading icing sugar all over the floor. 'What?'

Mandy gave her an amused look before she moved and Hunter walked into the kitchen. Mandy was right; he did look bad. There were dark circles under his eyes, his hair was a mess, and, though not creased, his clothes looked untidy. Autumn's stomach flipped nevertheless, her heart joining in.

'You've had an interesting morning,' Hunter said, his quiet voice steadying her for alarming reasons.

'A hellish morning,' she corrected. 'What are you, um, doing here?'

'Helping.'

'You brought Eli?'

'We're a package deal.'

Autumn absorbed that piece of information. Then her eyes moved to Mandy. 'You called him?'

'No, and clearly you didn't either.' Mandy grinned. 'He must be a gift from the universe.'

Hunter's lips curved into a half-smile. 'I'll keep an eye on things out here.'

They were both gone before Autumn could fully process the conversation. She shook her head, and went back to making the icing. When it was done, she turned her attention to the cake. She removed all the damaged parts and reassembled the three tiers. Then she filled a piping bag and played with different star tips as she tried to fix the spoiled fondant moulds between the tiers.

When she was satisfied, she took a step back. It wasn't noticeably different from the original design—she hoped—and would have to do considering the time constraints. Next she focused on the cascading flowers that had run from the top layer of the cake to the bottom. Half of the flowers were missing since they'd been made of gum paste and had cracked or broken during the fall.

She searched the kitchen for replacements, but could only find three. Sighing, she used some leftover fondant and flattened and folded, adding layer to layer, making small flowers and bigger ones, before setting them aside. When she thought she had enough, she checked the time.

She'd been busy for over an hour. Felt it in the stiffness of her upper body. Figuring she could take a quick break while the fondant settled from her manipulation, she popped out of the kitchen. Her eyes moved over the small bakery café. When nothing jumped out at her, she turned to Hunter.

'You're doing a good job.'

'Are you checking on me?'

'No,' she said with a small smile, 'I'm taking a break.' Her eyes lowered to the pram Hunter was rocking back and forth. 'He's sleeping?'

'Has been since I put him in the car to come here.' Hunter rolled his shoulders. 'It's the only thing that puts him to sleep.'

'Did you ask Grace about it?'

'No.'

She waited for more. Nothing came.

Not your business, Autumn, she warned herself. Found herself speaking anyway.

'Why not?'

'He's off his schedule.'

She forced herself not to react. 'So you didn't want to ask because…'

'She might ask about the schedule.'

Now she stopped herself from rolling her eyes. With a little sigh, she asked, 'Have you eaten yet?'

'No.'

'A grilled cheese and bacon sandwich?' It was his usual order. 'I can throw in a smoothie?'

'Just the sandwich. Wouldn't mind a soft drink. Something with caffeine.'

'Coming right up.'

She gave the order to the kitchen, took out two soft drinks and settled opposite Hunter at one of the free tables in the bakery. He was still rocking the pram.

'I'm sure it'll be fine if you stop doing that.' She nodded her head in the pram's direction.

'How do you know?' he asked.

'Surely you've tried?'

He shook his head. 'I don't want to. What if he wakes up?'

She stared at him. 'You put him back to sleep?'

'Another car ride?' He shook his head again. 'I'm tired of driving.'

'So you came here?' she asked. 'An hour's drive from your house?'

He blushed. For the life of her, she couldn't figure out why.

A part of her wanted to offer her help. He looked so tired, and his arm must have been going lame. But she didn't. She didn't know what kept her from it—or asking about how things were going with Eli—but a small flicker of pride sparked inside her because of it. Then, shame.

'Thank you,' she said. 'You didn't have to step in.'

'I got to distract myself from how tired I am by glower-

ing at a man who couldn't decide how he wanted his eggs.'
Hunter shrugged. 'I should be thanking you.'

She laughed uneasily, her mind telling her not to fall
into the trap of asking him why he was tired. But the trai-
torous organ abdicated before it could warn her against
the memories.

When Hunter had visited over the weekends, she'd
spend her Saturdays at the café and he'd join her. Usually, he'd do his own work, but on occasion he'd settle in
the kitchen, content with just watching her.

She'd grown used to it during their relationship, especially in the kitchen. It didn't matter if it was at her place
or his; at the bakery or her parents' house. He didn't seem
to care that there were better things to do. He would simply sit and watch her go through the motions of doing
something.

It had been unnerving at first.

She'd thought perhaps he was waiting for her to do
something wrong. It had made her clumsy. After she'd
had to toss out ingredients for a recipe she knew like the
back of her hand, she'd told herself to get it together. She
wanted people to see her, didn't she? To value her? That
meant people had to watch her.

It still made her anxious. And the anxiety angered her.
She was tired of worrying about what other people would
see when they looked at her. She didn't want to anticipate
the failures they'd see in her in case she had to defend
them. She wanted to stop comparing herself and finding
herself lacking. She'd done it with her sister. In a weak,
disgraceful moment, she'd done it with Grace.

Her face burned at the memory of it. How, in a vulnerable moment in his driveway, she'd revealed it to Hunter.

'What's wrong?' he asked her.

'Nothing.' She breathed a sigh of relief when they were
interrupted by their food. When the waiter left, she said,

'I'm assuming the universe didn't really send you here to help today.'

He looked amused. 'No.'

'Why are you here, then?'

The blush returned, though now she could see the tension around his eyes, his lips. He didn't answer her, and they ate their meal in a terse silence. Hunter kept rocking Eli's pram, with his foot while he ate and then again afterwards with his hand.

'The store's closing in half an hour,' she told him when they were done. 'It'll probably take me another hour to finish up here and then I'll have to deliver the cake.'

She was about to tell him he should go but another thought popped into her mind.

'Oh.'

'What?' Hunter asked.

She looked at him. 'I forgot I have to take this cake to the venue.'

'But you said—'

'No, I mean I'm going to have to see people. I can't go looking like this.' She gestured down to the black pants and top she wore beneath the apron she'd forgotten to take off. 'I'll get there the same time the guests will, probably.'

'I don't see a problem.'

'Of course you don't,' she said, amused despite herself. 'But seriously, I went to high school with the bride. Her in-laws only agreed to hire me because I'm a Bishop.' The eye-roll she gave was less humoured. 'I'm going as an heiress, not an entrepreneur.'

'You have time to change, don't you?'

'Yeah, but I have to close up and—'

'I'll do it.'

'Are you sure?' she asked. 'You have Eli.'

Hunter looked over at the sleeping baby. Automatically, Autumn did, too. She hadn't realised she'd been avoiding looking at him until that moment. Her subconscious must have known what those puckered lips, sucking on a non-existent dummy, would do to her.

'He still seems okay.'

'Hunter…' Her voice had softened. 'You don't have to do this.'

'Let me help. Please.'

It sounded as if he was begging, and it hit her in the gut. She stood up, then surprised herself by kissing his cheek. 'Thank you.'

She returned to the kitchen, refusing to think about what had just happened. Instead, she focused on the cake. True to her prediction, it took an hour to finish. She stood back, examining the end product. She thought she might have pulled it off. The comments her staff made as they trailed in and out of the kitchen, going through the end-of-day routine, seemed to support that thought.

But the real test was when she called Hunter to see it. He had no decorating experience, and yet felt the need to comment on her work whenever he could. Usually, it annoyed her. Today, she needed it.

'So?' she asked when he stood staring at it. Eli had woken up, and Hunter was giving him a bottle as he examined the cake. She ignored the adorable scene, kept her eyes on Hunter's face. 'Is it good enough?'

'No.'

Her face fell. 'No?'

'Not good enough, no.' He turned to face her. The air around them changed as she took in his expression. 'Just good. Perfect, in fact.'

Her heart exploded in her chest. They stood, staring at one another for only heaven knew how long. Soon, Autumn felt herself leaning towards him, compelled by the stirring in his eyes; the answer in her belly. She thought about how, if she rose to her toes, she would be able to touch her lips to his and maybe that stirring would stop…

Eli pulled his head away from his bottle and let out a hoarse cry.

'It's okay,' she said, though Hunter hadn't apologised. 'I need to take a shower and change anyway.' She looked at the baby, face red from the tears. 'Are you going to be okay to lock up?'

Hunter rocked Eli, trying to comfort him. It didn't work.

'How about I just stay here and watch things, and wait until you can lock up?'

She nodded. 'I'll be quick.'

CHAPTER NINE

IT WAS THE least he could do considering all she'd done for him.

That was what he thought as he walked around the bakery, trying to get Eli to calm down. He had a terrible feeling that he was doing something wrong with his son. It was the only explanation he could come up with. Their interactions consisted mostly of feeding and changing nappies—a hell of a thing to have to learn based on Internet searches—and driving.

If it had come in any form of a routine, Hunter would have called it a win. It didn't come close to the schedule Grace had given him either. The fact that there *was* a schedule at all seemed to confirm he was doing something wrong. Combined with what today was, being unable to take care of his son had churned his stomach. And he'd found himself driving an hour to Autumn's bakery because he'd needed to.

Realising Eli wouldn't stop crying anyway, Hunter carried the cake Autumn had boxed before she'd left to his car, leaving Eli in the cooler shop. He returned quickly, his baby's throaty sobs tearing up his heart. He pushed the pram outside, locked up the bakery, and got Eli settled before driving the short distance to Autumn's house.

He drove slowly, as much for the cake's benefit as Eli's. The sobs turned into quiet moans, as they had for the past three days. Hunter parked in the shade, but left the car on so the air-conditioner could keep the cake cool. He took out Eli's car seat, knowing Eli would need to be changed, and knocked on Autumn's door. When there was no answer, he rang the doorbell. Eventually, he tested the door and found it open.

'Autumn?' he called, not wanting her to get a fright. 'It's Hunter. I'm downstairs. I locked up the bakery and brought the cake. I just need to change Eli.'

'Thank you!' she answered. 'I'll be down in a second.'

The blow-dryer went on, and he realised what had prevented her from hearing him. She was diffusing her curls, he thought, remembering the countless times he'd watched her do it. Almost as many times as he'd watched her in the kitchen.

It had always been one of his favourite activities to watch her work. She had a skill in the kitchen that was worth watching. An ease, a grace that made that skill seem second nature, as if it was a reflex she'd crafted over the years, like walking or driving.

When they'd still been together, he'd watched her unashamedly. Now that they were broken up, he did it on the sly, refusing to be robbed of the simple pleasure.

The disappointment that he hadn't been able to do it today faded the moment he saw Autumn at the top of the staircase. He'd finished changing Eli—at least he'd proved adequate at that—moments before, and was waiting for her. A strong wave of emotion settled over him. Primitive and too embarrassing for him ever to contemplate out loud.

He felt as if he'd been transported into a teenage coming-of-age movie. His mouth was dry as Autumn descended, his pulse throbbing heavily in his ears; in other parts of his body. Exactly like a teenage boy seeing his prom date for the first time.

Except Autumn wasn't his. Not in the way he wanted. She'd acquiesced to being his person, but he didn't think she knew the extent of it. Of how desperately he wanted to be *her* person. But he couldn't give her what she wanted. And, if he was being honest with himself, he didn't deserve to.

'What?' she asked when she reached him. She lifted a hand to her hair, pushing a stray curl into the mass of them at the back of her head. 'Do I not look appropriate for a wedding?'

He blinked. Realised he'd been staring. He swallowed. 'You look perfect.'

As he said the words, his eyes dipped over her again.

She wore a blue dress with thin straps and a V neckline, cinched at her waist. The skirt part was made from two pieces of material crossed over each other, reminding him of the wrap dresses she liked to wear. This design created a V at the front, too, revealing a solid portion of firm legs. He imagined the material could be nudged open, providing access to her thighs…

'Oh,' she said hoarsely.

The colour on her cheeks deepened so much he almost didn't notice she wore blush. The rest of her make-up was done perfectly. Her eyes looked more prominent, her lips fuller. Along with the gold earrings dangling from her ears, she looked…breathtaking.

She cleared her throat. 'Thank you.'

He nodded, though he couldn't take his eyes from her face. 'I have the car running outside with the cake.'

She smelled fresh, soft, like the field of flowers outside her house.

'Thank you.'

He nodded again, and forgot all attempts at acting normal.

He was standing so close he could see the triangle of freckles beneath her left eye. She hated it; had once complained that Summer had got an even spread of them and she'd got whatever had been left. But he thought it made her unique. Her uniqueness made her beautiful, and that beauty burned in his stomach.

He took a deliberate step back and tightened his hold on Eli, who had quietened and was staring at Autumn, too.

'Eli thinks you look good, too.'

Her eyes lowered to Eli, then softened, though Hunter didn't miss the caution there.

'May I?' she asked, opening her arms.

'Of course.'

He handed Eli over and she looked down at the baby. The lips he'd wanted to kiss seconds ago curved into a smile. Hunter shook his arms out—not because they ached from the effort of carrying his son, but because they'd wanted to pull her closer. Mould her to his body, so he could feel her softness. Explore how much of his body still belonged to her.

'He's quiet,' Hunter said then, distracted by it. Thankfully.

'Yeah,' Autumn cooed, holding Eli's hand. 'I think he likes me.'

Hunter didn't respond.

'Is that a problem?' Autumn asked softly.

'No,' he replied immediately. 'No, it's not.' He shoved away the unwelcome doubts; ignored the voice that said *I told you so.* 'Where do you need to take the cake to?'

She told him, though hesitantly, as if she was afraid of his response.

He gritted his teeth. 'I'll drive you.'

'Oh, you don't have to do that.'

'The cake's already in my car. You'll need help loading and unloading it.' He took a breath. 'And this is the quietest Eli's been outside a car since Grace left. He likes you. I want to give him as long as I can with someone he likes.'

'Hunter.'

He didn't know what she saw on his face as she said his name. Whatever it was had her nodding.

'Can you grab that?'

She pointed to her handbag and coat on a stand next to the door. He took them. As soon as they'd strapped Eli into the car, they were driving.

The start of the trip was quiet enough for Hunter to

take stock of his body. He felt as if he'd spent the day working out, and he hadn't even done anything significant. He didn't dare do the same for his mind. Instead, he tried to distract it.

'You make wedding cakes every weekend now, don't you?'

'More or less.'

'*More?* How do you do *more*?' he asked, navigating the decline of the mountain leading into Cape Town carefully, mindful of the baby and the cake. 'It's exhausting.'

She laughed. 'Maybe you're just exhausted.'

She was sitting in the back of the car, next to Eli. The cake was in front with him. He didn't dare look into the mirror to check her expression. He was afraid of what he'd see.

'We have timelines,' she continued after a pause. 'Everything happens according to a plan made well in advance.'

'You also have the café.'

'I'm running a business. You do it. You know.'

'Maybe I don't remember as well since I've been on leave with Eli.' He looked in the mirror then. Laughed at the look she gave him. 'Fine. It's a fair point.'

'We're both entrepreneurs,' she said. 'We have people depending on us. Not only those who work for us, but those who depend on the work we produce.'

'Except I have a second-in-command to lean on.'

'I have Mandy and my team.' The words were all he got for the next couple of kilometres. 'My father agrees with you. He wants me to give Mandy more responsibility. Or hire someone else to deal with the day-to-day running of the café.'

Surprise rippled over him at the statement. Autumn rarely spoke about her family. In fact, he'd first assumed they were estranged. She'd told him that her father had had an affair a while back, and it had caused some familial distance. He'd accepted that…until she'd introduced him to her parents and sister and he hadn't noticed the distance. At least not with Autumn and any of the members of her family.

He had noticed her fatigue after though.

'You spoke to your father about this?'

'He came around a couple of weeks ago. To check on his investment,' she added dryly.

'That's what he told you?'

'Not in so many words.'

'Why would you say that, then?'

'It's true.'

He didn't have to look at her to know she was shrugging. 'Why couldn't he be checking on his daughter?'

'Same thing.'

'No,' he said quietly. 'It's not.' He paused. 'I have a father who isn't interested in me or anything I do. He never comes around.'

'He didn't invest in your company.'

'Your father has enough money not to care about what you do with your business.' He let it sit. 'It does sound like he cares about you though.'

He'd always believed it. Saw it in the way her father interacted with her. His pride, his presence, both of which he'd never got from his own father. The former not ever, even when he'd taken Calvin's place with Janie's care; the latter not since his parents' divorce.

He wondered why Autumn had never been able to see it. Or why she told him she and her family weren't close when they still had dinners and she still attended parties and planned anniversaries—

'Autumn,' he said with a frown. 'Didn't you drive to Wilderness last weekend for your parents' anniversary?'

'Yes.'

'So you only got back…' He trailed off with a headshake. 'You should have chased me away.'

'When you came to my door in the middle of the night distraught?' she asked lightly. 'I don't think so.'

'You must have been exhausted.'

'I am. I was, I mean.'

He looked into the mirror, then dragged his eyes back to the road. 'You are.' He paused. 'You haven't been sleeping.'

'I've been sleeping,' she said defensively. She sighed. 'Not well.'

Is it because of what you said to me? That you think you weren't enough for me?

She hadn't answered him when he'd asked; he doubted she wanted to speak about it now. Especially when mentioning her father had reminded him of her relationship with her family.

But something told him what she'd said had something to do with that.

'You know…' He clenched a jaw when the words stuck. Deliberately relaxed it. 'I didn't have a child with someone else because I didn't want one with you. You know that, right?'

CHAPTER TEN

AUTUMN SUCKED IN her breath, just as she had when they'd been at her house. The question felt as intimate as her fantasy of him drawing her close, lining his body with hers. Close enough for her to remember what she was missing; what she'd never have.

His expression then had been intense, a combination of want and self-denial. It was intense now, too, based on what she could see in the mirror. But there was an emotion there that twisted her insides.

'You're not doing anyone any favours by feeling guilty,' Autumn said quietly, ignoring his actual question.

'It's hard not to,' he said, fingers tight on the steering wheel. 'I feel like I...' He hesitated. 'I feel like I cheated on you. Or betrayed you, at the very least.'

Me, too.

She pushed the words away. Knew she couldn't answer his question about whether she knew he hadn't wanted a child with someone else. She was apparently still working through it. It annoyed her that he was poking at a fresh injury, one that had had no time to heal.

'I won't try and change your mind about that,' she said slowly. 'One, because I can't tell you how to feel. Two, because it's unfair of you to expect me to.' She swallowed down the lump in her throat. 'Three? You need to focus on the present, Hunter. On the future. For the sake of your son.' She looked at the little boy who'd fallen asleep in his car seat, then out of the window. 'Guilt is a useless emotion.'

As was hurt, she thought, determined not to let the fingers of it fist around her heart.

Instead, her own fingers curled where her hand rested

on her knee. Stopping them, she spread them over the skin there instead, almost sighing when they automatically tightened and dug into her flesh. It was pointless trying to stop them. Probably just as pointless as the anger that had coated the hurt and caused the reaction.

To be fair, her anger wasn't entirely directed at Hunter. She was mostly angry at herself. Because the weakness she'd accused herself of having by being vulnerable was there, fluttering through her body. Her reluctance to accept her father's interest as genuine, ricocheting in her chest. Most of all, her inability to accept that Hunter's decisions didn't reflect on her taunted her. Reminded her of all the times she'd thought of her parents' actions in the same way.

Did their focus on turning Summer into the Bishop heir mean they didn't see Autumn as worthy? Had their urging her into the kitchen been an opportunity to get her out of their way? Did they bring her out to mingle at their parties to placate her?

Why am I treated differently? What am I doing wrong?

Those questions were there every time her parents would talk to her about Summer. Before the affair, it had been because Summer hadn't been open about her life. After, because Summer had distanced herself.

Autumn had been so frustrated that she'd once told her mother Summer didn't need their concern.

'Of course she does.' Lynette Bishop had tutted. 'She's not like you.'

In that, Autumn had identified the real problem.

You're not like her.

She'd carried that with her long before her mother had said the words. Long enough that it had formed her into a person who tried to please everyone she met. Because she might not have been Summer, but she could be better. She'd taken what Summer hadn't done—opened up to people, engaged with them, been interested in them—

and incorporated it into her own personality. She'd seen what people needed and given it to them.

She'd become more popular almost immediately. With her parents' friends and acquaintances, who'd *oohed* and *aahed* over their charming daughter. With her teachers, who'd seen a hard-working girl, and her peers, who'd seen her money. All the while, she'd been aware of the pretence. Of the shifting and the changing. But it hadn't mattered, because people had preferred *her*.

Not the people she cared about most though.

The anger had been there long before now. She couldn't deny some of it had been aimed at Summer. Her sister didn't deserve it. It wasn't Summer's fault that Autumn compared herself to Summer and found herself lacking. Or that their parents did.

But she'd let it keep her from seeing Summer's pain. After their father's affair, Summer had withdrawn from the family. Autumn hadn't had the same reaction. She hadn't been as hurt, more affronted for her mother's sake than anything else. Since her mother had worked through it, Autumn had moved on. She'd known Summer hadn't— hadn't understood why either—but she'd done nothing about it.

She should have pushed Summer to tell her why. To help her understand. But no, Autumn had only discovered the truth at her parents' anniversary weekend. She could do nothing about what her sister had gone through now.

That was the cost of comparison, she thought suddenly. It put her at the centre of every experience, even if it was only to highlight her mistakes, her faults. But it blinded her to other people's experiences. That blindness kept her from acting. In this case, it had kept her from reaching out to her sister. What else had it kept her from doing?

Before Autumn could stew about it, Hunter spoke.

'I didn't mean to upset you.'

'You didn't,' she answered automatically. She bit the

inside of her cheek. 'Well, it's not completely you. I'm upset at myself.'

'Why?'

How could she phrase this? Her tendency to compare herself wasn't something she waved around, least of all to the people she cared about. What would they think about the mess that was her self-esteem?

She settled for describing the situation with her sister, leaving comparisons and her guilt out of it.

'Summer knew about my father's affair long before we did.'

She explained what had happened, including the events of her parents' anniversary where everything had come to light. She felt some of the pressure ease from her chest as the words spilled from her lips. He listened quietly, not interrupting once, not even for clarity. Not that she'd expected him to. Hunter had a singular talent for listening. No, for making her feel heard. For someone who felt as if she'd been shouting into the void her entire life, the experience was heady.

You're my person.

He was hers, too.

'You know it wasn't your fault,' Hunter said as he turned onto the road that would take them to the wedding venue. It was a long gravel path. Hunter drove slowly.

'You would say that.'

'Why?'

'Because you're my...friend.'

His cheek lifted in a smile. 'You hesitated.'

'No.'

The cheek lifted higher. 'Regardless,' he said after a moment, 'you couldn't have done anything about it. You didn't know.'

'I knew she was upset,' Autumn pointed out.

She looked out of the window again, at the fields that

stretched out on either side of the gravel road. There was a herd of cows in the distance. Five goats ate grass closer to them, giving them blank stares as they drove by.

'If I'd pushed her into telling me,' Autumn continued, 'she wouldn't have gone through it alone.'

'I see.'

She looked at him. 'What does that mean?'

He lifted a shoulder. 'Exactly what I said.'

'But *what* do you see, Hunter?'

'Well,' he said. 'Didn't you ask her why she couldn't move on?'

'Not in so many words.'

'But you checked on her.'

She nodded, though she didn't think he saw it.

'You encouraged her to make up with your parents?'

'Yes.' There was barely a beat before she added, 'But that was before I knew why she couldn't.'

'Because she didn't tell you.'

'Stop trying to make me feel better.'

He laughed. 'I'm trying to make you see the truth. Your sister chose not to tell you. She had the opportunity to.' His voice softened, all traces of amusement fading. 'You can't blame yourself for that, Autumn.'

'I can,' she muttered. 'I do.'

He laughed again, kindly, and pulled into a parking space close to the venue entrance.

'One question,' he asked as she unclicked her safety belt and peered into the car seat to check on Eli. As soon as the car had stopped, his eyes had popped open. She felt a wave of sympathy for Hunter's predicament.

'What is it?'

'Have you told her about this?' He waited as she pulled Eli out of the car seat. 'About him?'

She opened her mouth, but his expression told her he didn't expect an answer. He already knew what it was.

* * *

All things considered, the Thompsons responded well to the mess-up with the cake.

The bridal couple were still taking their photos, so perhaps that was a premature evaluation. But based on the reaction of the groom's parents, Autumn's friend's in-laws, the couple wouldn't care too much. Not if they were similar to the Thompsons in any way.

They were the kind of people who enjoyed dropping names. Hunter knew this because within the first ten minutes after being introduced, they'd mentioned the caterers, who were from a five-star hotel; Mel's dress designer, who was from a well-known international design house; the specialised wine for the day, which was produced by an in-demand local vintner; and, of course, the cake.

Having Autumn Bishop, heiress and owner of a wildly popular bakery, make the cake had softened the blow. Having her deliver it personally, where all the guests could see her, could mitigate any mistake. Having *#BakeryBoyfriend* deliver said cake with Autumn, he was stunned to learn, earned them an invitation to the wedding. Even with a baby.

'Oh, Mr and Mrs Thompson, we couldn't,' Autumn said with a polite smile. 'We couldn't impose.'

'Oh, you're not imposing.' Mrs Thompson waved a hand. 'There's more than enough space.'

She gestured to the venue, which was currently only half filled with guests. Since the bride and groom hadn't arrived yet, this seemed about right. Hunter assumed she wasn't pointing out attendance though. No, she was showing them the vast amount of space that would allow them to join the wedding as guests.

He supposed in some circles, this would be impressive. The round tables that filled the area, leaving enough room for a forest of trees—or so it looked like—to line each of the walls. Expensive chandeliers hung from the

roof, over a dance floor that had been raised from the
ground with insignia embossed into wood. He assumed
it was the couple's initials, but considering the way Mrs
Thompson was beaming, he wouldn't be surprised if she
told him it was hers.

'It's lovely, but we can't.' Autumn spoke firmly, though
there was a lyricism to the words that made Hunter wonder if she was truly rejecting them. 'We have the baby.'

Mrs Thompson peered at Eli, who was being traitor-
ously quiet in Autumn's arms. 'Is it yours?'

'He,' Autumn said deliberately, 'is not.' There was a
slight beat before she continued. 'I think we'll wait for
Mel and Ed outside.'

'Well,' Mr Thompson said when his wife looked at him
in panic, 'at least have a drink on us?'

'Of course,' Autumn said smoothly. 'Do you honestly
think we wouldn't take advantage of that gorgeous bar?'

The compliment seemed to soothe any ruffled feathers,
and soon he and Autumn were walking to the outdoor bar.

'Good work,' he said softly, manoeuvring Eli's pram
as he followed her.

She angled her head back, offered him a smile. 'Thank
you. It's a gift.'

He chuckled. Though he knew she was teasing, she
was right. Autumn had a gift. It wasn't charm as much as
a deep understanding of how people wanted to be treated.
How they needed to be treated. He supposed there was a
certain kind of charm in that, not that he'd ever be able to
understand it. He understood it in Autumn though. She
cared about people. Whether it was her ex-boyfriend-
turned-friend or her sister, she would rather hurt herself
than the people she loved.

Cared about, he corrected instantly. She didn't love
him. That part of their lives was over. It would do neither
of them any good to think otherwise.

When they reached the bar outside, Hunter saw Autumn hadn't merely been charming the Thompsons. The bar was genuinely beautiful. It looked as if it had been carved out of porcelain; white, glossy, with intricate patterns that looked as if it belonged in a museum. It seemed like a waste to have it at a wedding.

'Did you know this was here?' Hunter asked, standing next to Autumn.

'Yeah.'

She turned to him. She was directly under him, forcing her to look up and him to look down. Exactly as they'd need to if they wanted to kiss.

Fortunately, Eli kept that from happening.

Fortunately.

'I've been here before.' Was it just him, or did her voice sound breathy? 'It's one of those places rich people like having their events at.'

'Are you talking about yourself?' he asked, his eyes disobediently dipping to her lips. 'Or the people in your circle?'

'My parents' circle,' she said.

When he dragged his gaze up, he saw that hers was on his mouth. Her lips parted, and it took all his strength not to dip his head and taste her. As if she'd realised the danger, her head snapped up, and she shifted away, pulling Eli closer to her body before turning to the barperson.

He didn't think she'd known that the woman had been there, more that it had been blind hope to escape whatever web of attraction they were in. But she ordered herself a juice, and gestured for him to make his own order. He stuck with water.

'You could use something stronger, I'm sure,' she commented as the barwoman readied their drinks.

'So could you.'

'Yes, but Eli.'

The simple reason had his entire chest quaking with emotion. 'You still could,' he said determinedly. 'Eli means *I* can't drink. Plus, I'm driving.'

'Yet he's falling asleep in *my* arms.'

She gave him a catlike smile that told him she wouldn't entertain the conversation further. Which was good. He didn't want to thank her for helping his son sleep when it felt like verbalising his failure. He knew how exhausted Eli must be. The brief moments of sleep Eli had managed in the car couldn't have been enough. Disrupting his routine must have had a hell of an effect, too.

So it made no sense then that Hunter was thinking about leaning forward and teaching her what that smile would bring her.

Relief pacified some of the ache in his body when the bartender handed him their drinks. He took both of them gladly. It gave him something to do with his hands. The distraction of it gave his mind something else to focus on.

And yet, when she turned, his eyes dipped to the curve of her shoulders, the slope of her back, her butt, her legs. He swallowed.

'He's asleep,' she said softly. 'I think it means we can put him in the pram.'

'He usually wakes up,' he protested, but she was already lowering Eli into the pram, strapping him in. Hunter held his breath, waiting for the inevitable screech. It didn't come.

Of course.

'Come on,' she said so brightly he didn't have an opportunity to be upset about it. 'I want to show you something.'

'What?' he managed to ask, handing her the drinks when she gestured for them. Then she was walking beyond the boundary of the patio outside the venue, ignoring his question, and he had no choice but to follow her with the pram.

This is not a good idea, a voice inside his head scolded. It was the voice that had kept him out of trouble in school when he'd been tempted to use his fists to let out his frustrations about what had been happening at home. His anger at the injustice of losing the little girl he loved more than anything else. Anger he'd neatly aimed at his father.

Surprised by the thought, he tried to shake it off. The point was that that voice had kept him out of trouble. It had encouraged him to keep his head in the books. To expel his energy by exercising in the safety of his backyard.

It was a good, old friend. A trusted friend. Not one he should ignore because another, more tempting voice was cheering him forward.

He ignored it.

The two of them walked together wordlessly, the only sound the rattling of the pram against the narrow gravel path. Thick trees lined it; more stood tall in the distance. Because of the silence, the further down the path they walked, the clearer he could hear the trickle of water. It was louder before long, and she offered him a delighted smile as they turned a corner.

'Ta-da!' she said, opening her arms.

He smiled before he saw what she was showing him. When he saw, his lips stilled. It was a waterfall, which he'd gathered from the sound. But he hadn't expected it to be this beautiful.

The water gushed out of cracks in a mountain-like rock formation, with greenery bursting through random parts of the rocks. It flowed into a large body of water, then trailed further down into a narrower part that disappeared between the trees. The water was clear enough for him to see brown pebbles and an occasional sliver of colour indicating fish.

'Why haven't I heard about this place before?' he asked, checking that Eli was still asleep before he lowered to his haunches and stuck his hand into the water.

It was cool, refreshing, alerting him to how heated he was. He was tempted to throw off his clothes and dip his entire body into it. But he could only imagine what having fewer clothes on would tempt him into doing.

'Do you know of all the beautiful places in Cape Town?' she asked, putting their drinks a short distance away before lowering herself beside him.

When he realised she was going to sit down on the grass, he pulled her up enough to stop the momentum of her action. He sat, legs stretched out in front of him, and pulled her over his lap. By the time she reacted, she was already sitting on him.

'Hunter,' she said, sounding scandalised. His lips twitched. 'What are you doing?'

'I didn't want you to stain your dress.'

'Staining your pants is better?'

'I don't have to speak to clients soon.'

'Oh.' The righteous indignation deflated out her body. 'Thank you, then.'

She sniffed.

He hid his grin. 'You're welcome.'

She shifted on his lap, getting comfortable, and he thanked the heavens he'd thought to put her across his thighs instead of on top of him. If she'd moved like that there...

He swallowed, trying hard to act like the grown man he was and not the teenage boy she made him feel like. As if in answer to that thought, his eyes dipped to the curves of her breasts, and his mouth began to water, as if he could taste—

'Hunter?'

His eyes lifted, and he blushed. He should just hide in the water while he still had his dignity.

Because hiding would be so dignified.

'You're still not answering me,' she said softly, amusement dancing in her voice.

'What did you say?'

'I asked whether this is comfortable for you.'

'No,' he said immediately. She gave a sparkling laugh that had his lips curving.

'It was your idea.'

'I regret it.'

She immediately stiffened. 'Do you? I can—'

'Relax,' he told her, resting a hand on her thigh. 'I was joking.'

She looked down at her thigh, at his hand, and turned her head to his. Her eyelashes fluttered.

'No, you weren't.'

He didn't know if the trickling water had made him feel romantic. Or her proximity. Or the fact that she was looking at him as if she didn't want to move. But he said, 'No, I wasn't.'

CHAPTER ELEVEN

TERRIBLE IDEA, AUTUMN. This is a terrible idea. You can't undo this once you do it. Stop. Save yourself.

Her brain was being very logical with these thoughts, these observations. Problem was, she didn't want logic. Not when Hunter was looking at her as if he were hungry and hadn't eaten in years. If she were the food, she supposed that scenario wasn't entirely untrue.

Well, he was about to feast now.

They closed the distance at the same time. Autumn's hands lifted and gripped his face; Hunter's arms circled her waist and pulled her closer to him. Then they were kissing. Deeply, desperately.

His lips were soft, familiar, and knew exactly how to move against her so that all the blood pooled to the pit of her stomach. He angled his head as his tongue swept into her mouth, and she groaned, then pushed even closer to him. She was dimly aware of her skin shooting out in goosebumps; her breasts tightening; the rest of her body aching.

She knew, too, that they were going too fast. Their mouths were fused so urgently. Their hands were moving recklessly now, too. Hers eagerly ran over the bumps of his shoulders, the muscles of his back. They gripped the material of his shirt when his mouth left hers and found her neck, kissing and suckling on that spot where her neck met her shoulder that he knew drove her crazy.

'Hunter,' she gasped, even as she tilted her neck, exposing the skin to him. 'Stop.'

He immediately did, rearing his head back. His eyes were dark, hungry, fierce, and it sent a pang of desire through her already over-stimulated body.

'This isn't a good idea.'

He swallowed. Nodded.

'We should do it again. Slower. So we can enjoy it more.'

His gaze flew to hers, his eyes crinkling, and he leaned forward. She laughed, pulling back.

'Standing.'

Seconds later they were both standing. They stepped away from the drinks they'd miraculously managed to avoid knocking over during their passion. Now they stood, centimetres away from one another, staring.

'You're having second thoughts,' he said softly.

She laughed as a ball of nerves dissolved in her stomach. 'Aren't you?'

'Yes.'

She lifted her eyebrows. 'Then why are you asking me this?'

'I won't take advantage of you.'

Her lips curved. 'What if I want you to take advantage of me?'

She closed the distance between them, placed her hands at the top of his shoulders, before sliding them down to his chest.

His hands closed over hers, keeping her from moving lower.

'You want me to take advantage of you?'

'Like this,' she clarified. 'Yes, I do.'

'Autumn, I don't want...' He paused, his brow furrowing with intensity. 'I don't want you to feel like you...'

She waited, but he didn't finish it.

'Hunter,' she said softly, 'we both know this can't go beyond this moment.'

The frowned deepened. She wondered how she could find it cute.

'But we have this moment,' she continued with a slight

shake of her head. 'I, for one, would like to use it more productively than—'

His lips on hers silenced her, and she smiled into his mouth, then moaned when his tongue touched hers again. He'd dropped his hands, allowing her to make better use of her own. She ran them over his shoulders, down the thick curves of his biceps, his forearms, before taking his hands that had fallen to his sides. Thinking they were going to waste there, she moved them both to her hips.

Immediately, his hands gripped her flesh, squeezing, kneading, before they slowly moved up to her waist. Her skin shot out in gooseflesh again, unsurprisingly. His mouth was doing sinful things to hers, nibbling and nipping and coaxing; his hands imprinting on her skin.

He pulled away from her then, though not enough for their embrace to lose intimacy. One hand lifted to her cheek, his thumb brushing over the skin there. His eyes moved over her face swiftly. Seconds later, they did so more deliberately. The first felt as if he were checking for something; the second, as if he were committing it to memory.

It changed the air. It had been static and frenzied, even when their kissing had grown slower; now it felt heavy with meaning. Emotion.

His gaze met hers. 'You're the most beautiful woman I've ever seen.'

She'd heard the compliment before. Hell, she'd heard the compliment from *him* before. But it had never felt this…charged. Or life-changing. Her heart tightened in her chest, as if, with those words, he'd reached inside and grasped it, holding it firm in his hands.

Heaven only knew why that had her reaching for him again.

She pressed her lips to his, gave him a hard kiss before she dropped her head to his chest. She felt his hesitation before his arms closed around her, drawing her against his body.

She missed it. The raw, sexy passion of kissing him and the soothing emotion of being in his arms. She missed how she felt like the only woman in the world when he touched her, and how, when they were like this, she truly believed he thought she was the most beautiful woman.

Most of all, she missed loving this man. She missed imagining a future with him.

In that future, she didn't have to try so hard. She didn't compare herself to others. Wasn't changing herself to be like others. She was enough for him. She was enough for herself.

But that future was a fantasy. Reality was that she did compare herself to others. She did everything she could to make them like her. It meant she hated a part of herself—*that* part of herself—since it was the cause of her feelings of inadequacy.

Reality was that she didn't have a future with Hunter. She'd tried to have one with him, tried so incredibly hard. But it didn't change that he didn't want her. Not enough to even consider a compromise for their future together. Or even a *conversation*. No, he shut down or gave her the thinnest answer.

She could see it now. She understood it. As clearly as she saw and understood that her own issues had been an obstacle to their future, too.

The fact that he hadn't wanted a family had spoken to her fears of not being good enough. Her mind had screamed he hadn't wanted a family with *her*; the rest of her had accepted it. Had used Eli's existence as proof of it. Except now, that didn't seem like an adequate explanation. Hunter had turned to *her* after discovering he had a son. He'd asked *her* for help. Why would he do that if he didn't believe her good enough?

But she was so used to blaming herself. Faulting herself.

She was tired of it.

Perhaps it was that fatigue that helped her see she'd left Hunter for reasons other than what she'd told herself. She'd wanted a family and he hadn't, yes, but she'd wanted him more. A part of her had known that even then. So maybe, beneath that, she'd simply recognised that, just like with her family, she would have always felt second best with him.

His fears would come first.

She couldn't fault him for it. His trauma was significant. He'd lost a sister, someone he'd cared for deeply. Someone he'd taken care of. His parents had fought all the time, then divorced. Even before that, his father had been emotionally absent. People didn't just get over things like that. They had to work through it. But he barely acknowledged it. He kept it all bottled up inside. It would cast a shadow over everything he did. Just like what had happened with Summer. Just like…

Just like what she was doing to herself.

She stepped out of his arms. The look he gave her in response was inscrutable. It told her he knew something had happened in her head. She wasn't sure if it was because she had it written on her face, or because he knew her so well. Or a combination of both, since if she did have something written on her face, he would be able to read it.

She scooped down and collected her juice, downing it. The sugar seared its way down her throat, sizzling as it settled in her stomach. She wished she had another one. She wished she could drown herself in the sweetness so that she could burn off all the emotion that suddenly felt as if it were written on her skin.

As she made her way back up the path, she didn't wait for Hunter to follow her. Nor did she check that he was, though she didn't have to. She could hear the pram behind her. Knew his big, sexy body was easily handling both the piece of equipment and the awkward incline of the path. Unlike hers, she thought, her heels dipping into the ground for the fourth time.

If he says anything about it, she stewed, when she heard him take a breath behind her. But he must have changed his mind because no words were spoken. When she heard the breathing again, she realised he'd simply caught up with her. Grunting, she pushed forward, only to have a low-hanging branch thwart her.

She'd missed it, her gaze being on the ground ahead of her, and she'd walked directly into it. She felt a scratch against her forehead, but the real problem came after, when she tried to move and the branch got caught in her hair. Her first reaction was to pull forward, which did nothing, though she did hear a crackle that told her she'd break her hair if she kept pulling.

'Stop,' Hunter said before she could still.

'I was going to,' she mumbled.

He made a non-committal sound and stepped in front of her, examining the situation. She kept her eyes down, but he was standing so close that she could only see the torso she'd run her hands over minutes before. She lifted her gaze to his throat, but that reminded her that she hadn't kissed it when she'd had the chance. She knew what would happen if she looked higher, if she saw his lips, or his cheeks, or his eyes, so she closed her own and waited for it to be over.

It only succeeded in sharpening her other senses. It reminded her that she'd forgotten to hold her breath. Now she was forced to inhale Hunter's scent mixed with the earthy smell of the trees. She switched to breathing through her mouth, but somewhere in her mind she knew she'd always remember that potent combination. Already knew she'd smell it in her dreams.

She nearly sobbed.

'It's done,' he said seconds later, smoothing down her hair.

She opened her eyes, but he hadn't moved. He was studying her again, though this time he hadn't managed to keep his expression unreadable. She knew exactly what she saw there: regret.

Heat flushed her face as Hunter stepped back. She mumbled a 'thank you' before walking past him, pressing her lips together when they started trembling.

No, she commanded herself. She would not cry. She would not think about the kisses. In fact, she would pretend they hadn't happened. If she did, she could pretend the rest of it hadn't happened either. She would happily be able to ignore that she'd allowed her insecurities to taint every relationship, every decision she'd made in her life. And that she wanted Hunter, still, but couldn't do a damn thing about him not wanting her.

When they reached the patio, she heard laughter. Three steps later, she saw the wedding party outside the venue, enjoying a drink.

'Autumn!' Mel said, spotting her. 'Ed's parents mentioned you were here somewhere! They said something about the cake?'

'Yes, though let me first say *wow*! You look stunning, Mel,' Autumn said, examining the sparkly dress, feeling her heart vibrate as she did. 'Your eyes must have spun back in your head, Ed.'

Ed pushed up his glasses with a grin. 'Pretty accurate description.' He looked lovingly at his new wife.

'So,' Autumn said with a small smile, not wanting to linger, 'there was an accident with your cake today.' She explained it as concisely as she could. 'It won't be exactly what you expected, but I still think it's special.'

'Well,' Mel said, exchanging a look with Ed, 'we've actually seen it. My mum sent me a photo as soon as it arrived.' She paused. 'We love it!'

'You do?' Autumn asked, relief bursting in her chest. 'Oh, I'm so glad.'

'You shouldn't have been worried,' Mel replied, squeezing Autumn's shoulder. 'We love all your designs. And this still has everything we wanted, but it's somehow better.' She shimmied her shoulders in excitement. 'We can't thank you enough.'

'I'm glad you like it,' Autumn said. 'Though I'll still offer you a free cake on your first anniversary for the trouble.'

Mel and Ed's eyes widened.

'Oh, you don't have to do that.'

'I know I don't *have* to,' Autumn said. 'I want to.'

'Thank you,' Mel said, blinking. She beamed up at Ed. 'And I thought this day couldn't get any better,' she told him dreamily.

Ed grinned. 'Thank you, Autumn. We appreciate it.'

'Don't mention it.'

'Can we entice you to stay?' Ed asked after a beat. 'My mum told me she invited you—' his eyes shifted to behind Autumn '—and your boyfriend.'

Autumn stepped to the side, startled that she'd forgotten about Hunter. More so by the fact that Ed had called Hunter her boyfriend.

'Um, sorry. This is Hunter,' she said, though she knew it wasn't necessary.

Before Hunter could say anything, Eli let out an ear-splitting scream.

'Oh,' Mel said. 'I didn't realise you had a baby.'

'I don't.' Autumn forced a smile before waving a hand at Hunter, who'd started to reach into the pram. 'You have to drive,' she told him, picking up Eli. She figured after how long he'd slept, he either needed food or a diaper change. Probably both. 'As you can see, we really can't stay. But thank you.'

'Oh, yes.' Mel's frown deepened. 'Thank *you*.'

'Again, I'm sorry for the inconvenience. I look forward to hearing from you next year about the cake.' She stepped off the patio into the car park. 'It was nice seeing you again.'

She did a general wave, then followed Hunter to the car.

Neither of them spoke while she busied herself with changing Eli on the back seat. It took some creativity, but she managed. Soon he was in his seat, his little mouth suckling on a bottle of formula Hunter had had the foresight to prepare, and Hunter pulled out onto the road without a word.

But Eli calming down was bad for her brain. It meant she no longer had anything to distract herself with. Almost immediately she thought about how she'd wished she could have given a different answer to the Thompsons. To Mel. She wanted Hunter to be hers.

She wanted a wedding of her own. Thought of all the times she'd planned it in her head. Long before she'd met Hunter, admittedly. She'd walk into a wedding venue and wish for her own. Those desires had become more real when they'd been together. When a wedding, marriage, had been a possibility. But it wasn't now, so why had she still felt that vibration in her chest when she'd looked at Mel's dress?

And why was she wishing she could have given a different answer about Eli, too? He wasn't hers. He would never be.

'Have you spoken with Grace?' she blurted out, desperate to get away from the hopelessness.

'Yes.'

'*Spoken* spoken,' she clarified. 'Not messaged. Or emailed.'

His silence was telling. She let out a breath.

'Hunter, you can't run away from the fact that you're struggling.'

'I'm not.'

She lifted her brow when their eyes met in the mirror. He sighed.

'I don't want her to think I can't do this,' he admitted in a tight voice.

'You *can* do it.'

'Really? He hasn't slept in my arms once the last three days. Or quietened there, for that matter.'

She heard him damning himself in those words. She heaved another breath.

'Okay,' she said, though she knew it was a bad idea. But then, what was another one in the grand scheme of things? 'Let's go to your house.'

'What?'

'You need to stop being scared of your son, Hunter. I'm going to show you how.'

CHAPTER TWELVE

'YOU'RE SCARED OF HIM,' Autumn said for what felt like the millionth time. He gritted his teeth for what felt like the millionth time, too.

'I'm not scared of him,' he said. 'It's new.'

'It's not new. You took care of your sister.'

'I was six when she was born. I did the bare minimum when she was a baby.'

He wasn't actually sure that was true. He couldn't remember doing anything for Janie when she was a baby, though there was a high likelihood that he had helped in some way. His childhood up until the moment she'd died had been helping to take care of Janie.

His heart expanded in his chest, testing the limits of its confines. Seconds later, it shrank back to its usual size. The feeling stayed—expanding, shrinking—making him ill.

He wasn't upset about it. He'd expected some sort of physical reaction long before that moment. In fact, he'd expected it after his mother had called that morning.

'Are you okay?' she'd asked without preamble.

'Good morning to you, too, Mum,' he'd said.

Since he hadn't been able to sleep, he'd already been up, driving around Cape Town, trying to get Eli to nap. At that moment, Eli had been. Thankfully. Hunter wasn't sure how he'd explain the crying baby to his mother. He hadn't got to that point in his head yet. Hadn't been sure how he'd explain his one-night-stand baby to his mother.

'I'm fine. Why?'

'What do you mean "why"?' Her voice had lowered, as if she didn't want anyone to know what she was saying. 'Today's…you know.'

It had taken him too long to realise what she was talking about. When he had, he'd closed his eyes with a little breath.

'I'm okay,' he'd said after a moment. 'Are you?'

'Fine.' His mother had cleared her throat. 'I have the day planned out. No second free.'

'No second to think.'

'Which is the point,' she'd reminded him. Her tone had softened. 'You sure you're fine?'

'I am.'

When he'd disconnected, he'd taken a moment to let the shame flood his body. Then he'd driven directly to Autumn's place. He'd needed the comfort. Was embarrassed by how much. Not that it beat the embarrassment he'd felt at the fact that he'd forgotten the anniversary of his sister's death. Thirteen years ago, he'd lost Janie. And he hadn't remembered.

He wasn't sure why he hadn't remembered. His mother was a big enough part of his life that he'd noticed her absence in the past few weeks. She'd gone to Greece this time; she needed to be anywhere other than Cape Town, where Janie had died. She'd followed the custom every anniversary for the last twelve years. The first anniversary, she had been home, and still married. It had been rough enough that she'd finally filed for divorce.

The following year, she'd gone on her first overseas trip. Hunter had stayed at home alone since it had been during his final school year, and he hadn't been able to miss any days because of final exams. Besides, he'd preferred home over staying with his father, who he hadn't seen since the divorce.

Janie's illness had changed his father so much that he didn't seem to care about his healthy child. Hunter understood that distance now. He was doing it with Eli. When he'd seen how much better Autumn was at taking care of his son, he'd stepped aside and let her do it.

Was that how his father had felt? Inadequate and helpless? Or had he just been selfish? Caring about his own feelings more than he had Janie's?

If Hunter couldn't take care of his son now, when he seemed healthy, what would happen if Eli was sick? Would he put even more distance between him and his son? Would he follow in his father's footsteps and detach himself from the family?

'Hunter.'

His head moved in the direction of the voice, but it took some time to realise who was calling him. He had to figure out where he was first.

'Sorry.' He closed his eyes.

'Hunter.' Her voice softened. He opened his eyes again. 'What's wrong?'

'Nothing's wrong.'

'Something's wrong,' she dismissed with confidence. 'You're quiet.'

'I'm always quiet.'

'True.' Her lips curved. 'But you have different kinds of quietness. There's the normal, broody kind. Then there's the "something's wrong" kind. You're doing the latter.'

He wanted to laugh, but was afraid it would reveal the hysteria brewing inside him. 'You know me too well.'

'My curse.'

A curse. Now he did laugh. Then walked outside because he didn't want laughter to turn into tears. Shame, guilt, confusion sat like bricks in his throat. Then there was the grief, holding those emotions together like cement.

A curse.

He currently felt cursed himself. As if he couldn't do anything right for his son. Or in his life at all, he thought, remembering that he'd left Autumn inside the house without any answers. The fact that she was there in any capacity proved that he was doing something wrong. She didn't deserve to be dragged into this.

Except…he needed her.

That felt like a curse, too. Needing her so deeply but being unable to be with her. Not in the way he wanted. But this was safer. It was safer to let her take care of Eli, too. He wouldn't hurt them this way. He wouldn't lose them this way.

'Hunter.'

The voice was urgent at his side, and he turned, wondering how long she'd been there. And what she'd seen.

'Hunter,' she said again, edging closer to him. Her hands lifted and her thumbs brushed his cheeks. Only then did he realise tears had been falling from his eyes.

Damn it.

He stepped away from her, took a ragged breath. He was embarrassed at the vulnerability of it. The tears were an outward display of the turmoil going on inside him. He couldn't hide the tears as he did the turmoil. He couldn't hide that he was broken and hurting and his emotions made no sense.

'I'm worried about you,' she said, twisting her hands together.

'You shouldn't be. I don't deserve it.'

'Of course you do,' she said dismissively.

Her passion nearly made him smile; the concern made him want to give her something. Anything.

'The test,' he said quietly. 'It's on Monday.'

'This coming Monday?' she asked. He nodded. 'Oh.' Paused. 'Do you want to talk about it?'

He took a long time to answer. Mostly because until he'd mentioned it, he hadn't realised the test had been weighing on his mind, too.

'I keep thinking about what happens if Eli is sick,' he said slowly.

'What happens?'

'Where to begin?' He gave a humourless laugh. 'He'll have a tough life. I wouldn't know how to raise him.'

'In terms of his practical needs?'

'No. No, that I'd be able to do.' He knew that much. 'I… I want to be a good father. I'm not sure I can be if I end up spending my life trying not to be like my father.'

'Why would you be like him?'

'I have that gene inside me. Just like the CF gene I carry.' He took a breath. 'If Eli's sick, maybe that would trigger something inside me. The "Terrible Father" gene.'

She took the revelation in her stride. 'Is that why you're scared to take care of Eli?'

'I'm not—' He broke off on a sigh. 'Maybe.'

'Right.' There was a long pause. 'Did I tell you part of why Summer divorced Wyatt was because she was afraid he would turn into my father?' She was looking out onto the pool, her arms folded. The stance was so casual she might have been at a party. 'Another big reveal from the anniversary weekend.'

'I'm…not following.'

'I'm getting there,' she replied patiently. 'She never told Wyatt about it. She couldn't. It would have meant telling him about my father's secret, and she was paralysed by keeping it. So she asked for a divorce.'

He waited now, sensing there was a point.

'She gave up on the thing that made her the happiest because of my father.'

'Are you talking about us?'

She looked at him, the curves of her cheeks flirting with her eyes though it wasn't a smile she gave him. 'Not directly. Although if you are keeping Eli at a distance because of your father, you've done that with me, too. Before we broke up,' she clarified. 'You pulled away, put distance between us. It was how I knew.' Her gaze dropped for a second. 'But what I meant is that she allowed my father's actions to influence her own. His mistakes became her mistakes. She almost lost the love of her life because of it. I'm not saying that's what's happening here,' she said quickly, and, though it was dark, he could tell she was blushing.

'I know.' He waited a beat. 'You're saying to be careful not to let my father's mistakes become my own because I'm fixated on avoiding them.'

'Yes.' She paused. 'You have the power to change your life, Hunter. You can be a good father if you want to be. You only need to be yourself.' She tightened her arms around herself. 'But you need to stop using him as an excuse.'

He didn't bother denying it. He knew it was true. Had realised it early on in this experience. He'd even had empathy for his father after he'd struggled to deal with Eli; he had even more now that Autumn had outlined his own actions. His habits, it seemed.

When Hunter felt overwhelmed, he put up barriers. They protected him against other people's opinions. Their expectations. But they also kept out the support he needed, causing him to be so overwhelmed he ended up crying without even realising it.

As he thought it, panic rose inside him. It tossed out the other emotions that had been building up in his throat as it took residence there. As it choked him. It made no sense to respond this way to something that hadn't been a surprise. He'd known what Autumn had told him to some extent. Facing it in its entirety now was burdensome, but he shouldn't have been reacting like this.

Until he remembered the barriers had first been erected when he'd stepped in to help take care of Janie.

He hadn't wanted his mother to know how scared he'd been that he'd do something wrong. He hadn't wanted his father to know how angry he'd been at being put in the position of a parent when he'd still been a child. The barriers *had* become a habit. Not only to protect himself, but to protect those around him.

Except they had kept him from identifying his own emotions. Had boxed them in rather than out. Perhaps not all his emotions, but one very specific emotion. It came in waves at unexpected times. Had him clinging to the only person who could calm him, to the point that he'd redefined their relationship so he wouldn't lose her.

Grief.

He'd pushed it so far down that he only dealt with it subconsciously. He'd refused a chance at a family with Autumn because of it. He was keeping his distance from Eli because of it, too. His relationship with his parents had likely also been affected by it. The lack of a relationship with his father seemed to prove that.

But he didn't have time to wonder which other actions in his life had been driven by the emotion. Panic had given way to grief, and, with the barriers gone, nothing could protect him from the onslaught. He stumbled to the table, lowering his body to a chair as the pain saturated his body. Bracing his elbows on his thighs, he dropped his head into his hands, and shut his eyes when heat arrived at them in wave after wave.

He heard the sound of Autumn dragging a chair next to his, then felt the warmth of her arm around him. The weight of her head hit his shoulder, and blindly he reached for her hand, not in the least surprised when he found it.

In silence they sat as he waited out the grief. He didn't bother wiping at the tears. They came randomly, whenever a memory of his sister would stroll into his head. Her laughter echoed in his memories; that one askew tooth she'd had flashing before his eyes. She'd been happier than any kid he'd known. He'd fought for that. His mom had, too.

'Why are we turning it into a game?' he'd complained one day when his mother had encouraged him to play with Janie during her airway clearance therapy.

'So that it's not something negative for her,' his mother had replied. Her eyes had rested on him, and she'd lowered herself until they were face to face. 'This is the only life she knows, Hunter. We can make that life happy for her. You and me.'

He'd do the same for Eli, he thought fiercely. If Eli was sick, Hunter would make sure his son led a happy life. The vow felt like fresh air when all he'd been inhaling was smog. He'd told Autumn he wouldn't know how to raise Eli if he was sick, but now Hunter knew. He'd always known. He'd just…shoved it behind the barrier. But Janie had shown him. Perhaps it was time he allowed her to show him more.

He took a breath. Immediately, Autumn straightened. She started to pull her hand away, but stilled when he resisted.

'I didn't mean for that to happen,' he said.

'I figured.' She paused. 'What did happen?'

'Today's… It's the anniversary today.'

He didn't have to elaborate; she understood. Her grip tightened. It comforted his aching heart.

'Is that why you came to the bakery?'

'I needed the distraction.' From Eli, too, he thought, then frowned. 'Where is Eli?'

'In the pram.'

She gestured with her head. The pram was a few metres away from them. He hadn't even noticed.

'Is he sleeping?'

'He was when I put him down.'

He shook his head. 'I don't know how you do it.'

'By being relaxed,' she said softly, squeezing his hand before she let go and went to check on Eli. 'I think he senses your discomfort around him. Your fear,' she explained. 'I suppose I could have made that clearer earlier.'

'Maybe.' He paused. 'I was scared when I helped with Janie, too.'

She studied his face. 'Why?'

'I thought she might…' He trailed off when the emotion rose again. 'She did,' he ended lamely.

Her eyes widened, then her expression became unreadable. 'You can't let that affect you here.' Her tone was clipped, as if he were a disobedient student and she the teacher.

'Excuse me?'

'It's the same thing as with your father.' With each word, her voice got cooler. Detached. 'You can't raise Eli if you expect him to die.'

He winced, but his spine straightened. 'I…don't.'

'Good,' she said. 'Now, we can try again with Eli in the morning. For now, we rest. It's been a long day.'

'The morning?'

'Do you mind me staying over?'

His brain melted, but somehow he shook his head.

'Good. I'll spend the night with him. You get a good night's sleep.'

He opened his mouth to refuse, so he wasn't sure how he found himself in his bedroom shortly after. Or how he got through a shower, stumbled into bed, and fell asleep.

She was completely disorientated when she woke up. The room was dark, vaguely familiar and cool. Her brain noted this idly as it adjusted to being awake. It took longer to realise she was awake in Hunter's house.

She shot up, looking around more alertly this time. It wasn't the baby's room. She was in one of Hunter's guest bedrooms. The dark blue curtains had been drawn and the air-conditioning had been put on at a respectable temperature. Her body ached, and with a small groan she remembered the discomfort from the night before.

Eli wasn't a fussy baby, at least not with her. But he was still a baby and he woke up every two to three hours for a feeding and a change. After the work day she'd had the day before, the disruptions weren't ideal. After the emotional afternoon and evening she'd had, the disruptions were perfect. She didn't have to think about Hunter crying, or about the realisations she'd had as she'd told him about Summer's mistakes.

Her body on the other hand…

Autumn tried to remember where she'd fallen asleep. It must have been the armchair in Eli's room. She'd dozed in it all night, hence the aching body. But if she'd fallen asleep there, it must have meant Hunter had brought her here. Which also meant she'd been sleeping for far too long. Sighing, she got up, showered, and put on her clothes from the day before.

The smell of bacon hit her as she walked into the kitchen. When she saw the coffee pot, she suddenly smelled that, too. She was already drinking a cup when Hunter walked through the front door with Eli.

She frowned. 'Was he being fussy again? Did you have to take him for a drive?'

'Good morning,' he said mildly. 'No. We went to get you something to wear.'

'Oh,' she said, setting her cup down on the table as Hunter took Eli out of the pram. She was surprised to see him awake…and not crying.

'He's been okay?' she asked, resisting the urge to walk to Eli and snuggle him. It was surprisingly difficult. She didn't like the feeling it stirred in her belly, or the realisation that it stirred any emotion in her at all.

'He's been better.' There was a pause. 'I'm trying to take your advice.'

'Good.'

He took something out of the pram, then extended a hand to offer her a packet. She took it, wondering why things had suddenly become awkward. Was it because of what had just happened inside her? Or were they both trying too hard to pretend the day before hadn't happened?

'Thank you for buying this,' she said, determined to act normally. She would even pretend her insides hadn't turned into mush because he'd thought to buy her clothes. 'I'm not sure this is appropriate for daywear.'

'I wanted you to be comfortable.' He settled Eli in a baby bouncer on the dining-room table and went to pour himself a cup of coffee. 'I thought that would work.'

He gestured to the dress she'd removed from the bag. It was a red and white button-down polka dot dress. She shook it out, draped it over her front.

'It looks like it'll fit,' he said.

She checked the label. 'It's my size, so it should.' She slanted him a look. 'You remembered.'

He angled his head, but didn't comment. The rest of the packet contained white sneakers, socks, some toiletries, underwear... Top and bottom.

'Thorough.'

He shrugged, though she thought she saw a faint glow on his face. 'You're my guest.'

'Hmm.' She threw the dress over her arm and picked up the bag with her free hand. 'I'll go change.'

She did so quickly, pleased to find that most of the items fitted. The underwear was a size too small, though she didn't know if she could blame that on Hunter being optimistic about seeing her or—

No.

Right. She wasn't supposed to be thinking about that. Hunter wouldn't be seeing her in the too small underwear. Optimism wasn't an option. It wasn't as though either of them was hopeful they'd be making out and seeing each other without clothes. She certainly wasn't. She wasn't remembering how his mouth had felt when it had nibbled her neck right at that—

No.

Oops.

She smoothed down the front of the dress, poked her hair so that the curls didn't look as wild, then left the bed-room. When she found Hunter and Eli missing, she immediately went to the patio, unsure of how to feel about the fact that she knew he was there. They'd shared many Sunday mornings when she was off work doing exactly this. She was off today, too, but they weren't together, and it felt different.

'Do I pass inspection?' she said, walking in.

She did a quick twirl for him, throwing out her hands. When she faced him again, she found both father and son smiling at her.

'Oh,' she said with a little laugh. Her tummy jumped at Hunter's smile, but she focused on Eli's instead. 'Has he smiled before?'

Hunter looked at Eli. 'Not that I've seen.'

She twirled again, got the same reaction—just from Eli this time—and told herself she wouldn't do it for a third.

'Well, now we know,' she said before sitting down in front of the plate she assumed Hunter had prepared for her. 'How…er…how did you manage to do this all this morning?'

'I was operating on a good night's sleep for the first time in a while.'

She studied him. Saw that he wasn't only referring to the nights since he'd had Eli. She nodded, picked up her knife and fork. Deliberately, she cut a piece of bacon and toast, but found him looking at her before she could put them in her mouth.

'What?' she said when he didn't speak. 'Do I look funny?'

'You look charming.'

She almost choked on the food she'd been chewing, but managed to swallow down the bite before she said, 'Charming? What am I? Your grandmother?'

He chuckled. 'I've never seen you in something like this.'

She focused on her plate again. 'And yet you bought it for me. Why?'

'I don't know. I thought it would suit you.'

'Because I'm so charming,' she said dryly.

He grinned. 'Yeah.'

She rolled her eyes good-naturedly. 'I'm not charming,' she told him. 'Just good at giving people what they want.'

She continued eating her meal in silence. When she was done, he said, 'That's exactly what I thought yesterday after seeing you with the Thompsons. You have a gift.'

She sat back with her cup of coffee, holding it with both hands. 'I wouldn't call it a gift.'

'I would. You care about people. Enough to give them what they want.'

'That's a strange way to describe being a people pleaser.'

She was so stunned by the words that for a full ten seconds, she blinked rapidly. His wide-eyed reaction didn't even trouble her.

'That's how you see yourself?' he asked eventually.

She chewed on the inside of her lip. 'I suppose.' Then, realising she didn't want to restrain herself, she continued. 'I mould to people's expectations, Hunter. It's not a gift. It's a reminder.'

'Of what?'

'How inauthentic I am? How no matter what I do, I'm never good enough?'

She hated the garbage spilling from her lips. Didn't make it any less true.

'Did I...did I make you think this?' he asked.

She sighed. 'It's not just you. It's everyone. No matter what I do, people don't...like me.' She cringed.

His expression was alarmed, then transitioned into thoughtful. His eyes didn't leave hers; it felt as if he saw through her. Uncomfortable, she avoided his gaze, studying his garden. There were high walls enclosing the property, not allowing for a view of the surroundings as her place did. But inside the walls was spectacular enough that she could forgive him.

Bright flowerbeds lined the walls, with tall trees in every corner. It made the pool in the middle of the area seem like an oasis. The water sparkled in its blueness, tempting anyone who looked at it to jump into its depths. There was a bench just beyond the pool, directly opposite where Autumn was sitting, with enough grass in front of the pool, before the patio, for kids to run and have fun.

Eli would be happy here, she thought. Her heart ached, just a little.

'Autumn.' When she turned, Hunter's expression was unreadable. 'Why can't you see yourself the way other people do?'

There was a moment before a lump travelled to her throat and her eyes burned. Before the emotions weighed down her composure and she had to fight off tears. In that moment, she thought about the question—and had no good answer to give. The realisation devastated her.

'I know,' she said into the silence that extended. Of course he wouldn't say anything that would give her an easy out. His talent for making her feel seen had its downside: he *saw* her. 'Or rather, I *think*, there's a…discrepancy between how I see myself and how other people might see me.'

She thought about the day before, when she'd realised she saw other people's actions as a reflection on herself. And how she'd gone through her entire life allowing it to affect her decisions. Her relationships.

'I'm working on it.'

'Are you?' he asked quietly. 'How?'

'What do you mean how?' she retorted. 'How are you planning on telling your mother about Eli? I'm assuming you haven't.'

It was the first thing she'd thought of, but she regretted it as soon as she saw his expression.

'No, I haven't,' Hunter replied. 'It's not the right time.'

She blinked, then closed her eyes when she realised. 'I'm sorry. That was unnecessary.'

'But relevant.' His gaze was steady on her. 'I'd like to

tell her in person. After the test results come back so that I can have that answer for her.'

She silently groaned.

That's what you get for acting like a jerk.

'Can you tell me how you're working on it now?'

'Okay.' There was a beat. 'I...don't know.'

'Then let me make a suggestion.' It wasn't a question, but she nodded. 'When people show you how much they care about you, believe them.'

Those words echoed in her head as she excused herself to do the dishes. He'd protested, but had seemingly understood she'd needed the space when she'd insisted. She carried their plates and mugs to the kitchen, forgoing the dishwasher and washing the dishes manually.

It was soothing, the act of it. Made her feel useful, which distracted her from the way Hunter's advice had unsettled her.

Ha! a voice in her head said. A spokesman, she assumed, for the feelings she was trying to ignore. She tried to reason with it, though she was well aware of what that said about her mental stability. *You're messy*, she told it, hoping it would carry the message to the rest of her emotions. *Confusing and complicated and so damn messy.*

Reasoning didn't work, so she was forced to think about how he'd told her to do the one thing she had trouble with. Her self-esteem kept her from seeing the true motivation behind people's actions. And since she saw people's actions as reflections on herself, how could she take his advice?

She wanted to. Understood it in a way she hadn't before that weekend. The only answer she could come up with was that she had to work on the way she saw herself. But that seemed like an impossible feat. So impossible, she spent most of her menial task worrying about it.

CHAPTER THIRTEEN

'AUTUMN.'

Her head whipped to Hunter. 'What?'

'We're here.'

She looked around and saw that they'd arrived at her house. After she'd finished the dishes, she'd asked him to drop her off at home. Her mind was a mess and she was afraid of how much he'd see if she stayed there. So she'd pretended not to see his disappointment. Tried not to notice the tension in his body the entire drive home.

Now she was ignoring her own disappointment at the unwelcome thought that had popped into her head with his announcement of their arrival.

I'm going to miss you and Eli.

She grabbed the plastic bag she had her things in, and opened the door. 'Thank—'

He was already at the opposite side of the car, strapping a sleeping Eli into the pram.

'What are you doing?'

'We need to talk.'

'No.'

'No?'

'No,' she confirmed. 'We already talked. Now we—*I*— need some time to recover.'

'Okay.'

But he wheeled the pram around, stopping on the pathway to her front door. With a frustrated sigh, she joined him.

'I need a break from this,' she blurted out when she stopped in front of him. 'This is hard, Hunter. Harder than I thought it was going to be.'

'I know. I'm sorry.'

'No,' she said again. 'I don't want you to apologise.'

'What *do* you want?'

'I want… I don't know, Hunter. A bunch of things I can't have.'

'Me, too,' he admitted softly.

'Like what?'

'I see you with Eli and I… I wish it had been you.' His voice was as steady as ever, which annoyed her, considering he'd sent off an earthquake in her mind.

'This,' she said through tight lips. 'This is why it's so hard.'

'Autumn,' he said, taking a step closer. 'You've already helped me more than you can know. You're…perfect to me.'

'I'm not.'

He took her hand. 'How, then, do you make me feel like I'm capable of doing more than I think I can? You believe I can raise Eli and be a good father. It makes me feel like…' He trailed off and looked at their hands. 'I'll be holding onto that feeling for a long time. But you don't deserve to go through this. You deserve more.'

She didn't try to hide the tears burning in her eyes.

'Why?' she asked hoarsely. 'Why do I deserve more?'

'I just told you.' He paused. 'You steady me.'

'What does that matter when you don't want me?'

'What?' His voice was rough. 'Of course I want you.'

'You had me.' She shrugged. 'But your past was more important than your present. Or your future.'

'That's not fair.'

'No,' she agreed. 'But it is true.'

There was a long, drawn-out silence before he cupped her face.

'I'm sorry,' he whispered, leaning forward, kissing her forehead. 'It's not you.'

She couldn't believe him, but when he moved back, she lifted her hands and gripped his face.

'A goodbye?' she asked impulsively. Desperately.

His gaze dipped to the lips she'd wet with her tongue. It slid to behind her to check on Eli, then it heated and he nodded.

When their lips met, fireworks shot to the sky.

She resisted the urge to take and take so she could fill the part of her she knew would be empty once he left. She ignored the greed to make more memories, too. Hot ones, sweet ones, a combination. She ignored it all and focused only on the moment. On his mouth moving against hers.

As it always did, his kiss awoke parts of her body reserved only for him. The thrill of it started low in her belly, spreading out. Spreading down. She wanted to invite him into her house, to entertain her body now that it was awake. But she knew they shouldn't. So she settled for the warmth spiralling out in her abdomen. For the way her heart *pitter-pattered* in her chest.

She opened her mouth to his tongue, inviting it to plunder and claim. It did neither. It teased and it offered. It tangled with hers, gifting her memories with its sweetness, its gentleness anyway. Her breath was swept away with it; with the thought of that precious gift. Her body was swept away with the skimming of his fingers over her neck, her shoulders, the sides of her breasts.

She gasped when skimming became gripping. When his hands dug into the flesh of her backside and brought her against the hardness of his body. Her breath was already gone, but that took away any remnants there might have been. And feeling him against her, understanding the immensity of what she'd lost, caused her to pull back and pant for air.

'Inside. Now.'

The words had barely been said before he left her embrace and pushed the pram to her front door. Then he was back in front of her, lifting her up and finding her mouth again. She could stay like this for ever, she thought, his steps sending vibrations through her hyperaware body. Their mouths could be fused for all eternity. She would gladly sacrifice convenience for the sake of it. If it meant she could always feel this full, this light, this vibrant, she would sacrifice any convenience.

He fumbled with the doorknob, and she realised it was locked. Wrenching her mouth from his, she told him, 'Back pocket.'

He smiled and she kissed him again, because, damn it, that smile was sexy and confident and he was the hottest man she'd ever kissed. His hands slid into her back pocket, lingering, kneading, then he drew out the key and fumbled with the lock this time. But when the door swung open, he didn't move.

She moaned into his mouth, encouraging him, before she realised he'd stopped kissing her back.

'Hunter, what—?'

She stopped when his eyes shifted to behind her. Though she had no idea what she would see, she squeezed her thighs, gesturing that he put her down. He did, and she shifted so that she was in front of him when she turned, determined to cover the part of his body that hadn't yet got the memo that they'd been interrupted.

'Summer,' she said when she finally got her senses back. She was relieved it was her sister. It could have been worse. 'I didn't know you were back from the lodge.' She put her weight on her right leg. 'I...er...didn't see your car.'

'Wyatt dropped me off on his way into town,' Summer replied, coolly amused. 'I thought I'd spend some time with my sister, but clearly that was—' her eyes shifted to Hunter; the amusement deepened '—presumptuous.'

'Nonsense,' Autumn said, voice strangled. 'Hunter was just leaving.'

She turned and gave him an apologetic look. His expression was unreadable.

'Thank you,' he said. 'For everything.'

She clenched her hands to keep from reaching out to him. 'You're welcome.'

'I guess I'll see you...around.'

'Yes,' she said weakly.

'It was nice seeing you again, Summer,' Hunter said, politely.

'Same here.'

He nodded at Autumn before dragging the pram away and heading back to his car. She gave a small wave when he was done strapping Eli in, and worried when she felt as if she were waving off a part of herself. She was still staring long after he'd driven away, even when Summer came to stand beside her and put an arm around her shoulders.

'Was that a baby with Hunter?'

Autumn gave a hoarse laugh. 'Would you believe that you imagined it?' She leaned her head on Summer's shoulder, letting herself take the comfort her sister was offering.

'What happened?' Summer asked after a moment.

'A lot,' Autumn admitted. She straightened. 'If I'm going to tell you, let's go inside. I'd rather die of mortification inside my home than outside it.'

Summer laughed, and they went inside. Her sister headed directly to the kitchen. Autumn followed slowly, sliding onto the kitchen stool and plopping her head into her hands. She watched as Summer made them both a cup of tea, and would have been amused at the irony of it if humour hadn't been the last thing she was willing to feel.

Less than two weeks earlier, Autumn had done the same thing for Summer. Making her a cup of tea after Summer had seen her ex-husband, Wyatt, for the first time in two years. Tea solved a multitude of sins. It had been their philosophy long before they were old enough to indulge in it. She felt a surge of gratitude for her sister and their relationship, but guilt followed closely. She'd been jealous of Summer her entire life and her sister hadn't deserved it. Because of it—because of her own selfish feelings—Autumn hadn't been there for her sister when Summer had needed her.

Autumn sank her head down so that her chin rested on the kitchen table.

When Summer turned around, she laughed sympathetically.

'Oh, no, is it that bad?'

'Yes,' Autumn mock sobbed as she rested her forehead on the counter now, making the words come out muffled. 'Everything is too complicated and I can't—'

'Wind,' Summer interrupted, using the nickname she'd given Autumn when they'd been children. An ode to the season she'd been named after and the fact that Summer believed her to be a whirlwind of goodness. Autumn almost laughed. 'I can't hear what you're saying.'

She forced her head up. 'Sorry. I was saying that everything is complicated and I'm *tired*.'

Now Summer's laugh sounded sparkling. 'You sound exactly like I did at the lodge. In fact,' she said, picking up the two mugs and handing Autumn hers, 'after I told Wyatt I loved him, I also said I was tired.'

Autumn regarded her sister sullenly. 'And now you're well rested and it's all sunshine and roses.'

'I wouldn't say well rested...' Summer's eyes twinkled, and she ducked when Autumn threw a dishcloth at her. 'I'm sorry, I'm sorry.' She laughed. 'I couldn't resist!'

'Try harder.'

Summer straightened her face, then sobered for real. 'Okay.' She leaned over the counter, sipped from her tea. 'Tell me what's happening.'

'No.'

Summer tilted her head. 'I'm sorry?'

'I can't tell you what's happening until I apologise.'

She set her cup down, took Summer's out of her hands before threading their fingers together.

'I'm so sorry about what you went through, Sun,' she

said, using the nickname she'd given Summer in response to the one Summer had given her. 'I'm sorry I didn't see what it really was and push you to tell me more.' Her throat got tighter and tighter as she spoke, so her last words were said in a thin voice. 'I should have seen it. I should have suspected it. I was—'

'Wind,' Summer interrupted. 'You don't have to apologise. You didn't do this to me.'

'I didn't see it either.'

'Because I hid it. That was the entire point.'

'But I should have—'

'Why?'

'I'm your sister. Your twin sister.'

'Fraternal twins.'

'As if that makes a difference.'

Summer angled her head in acceptance. 'Doesn't change that you didn't do anything wrong.'

'I should have known.'

'Why do you keep saying that?' Summer asked. 'How should you have known? Why should you have known?'

'I told you—'

'That's not it though. Sisters don't know everything about one another.' She dipped her head. 'Have you told me everything about you, Wind? I think not. Or I wouldn't have opened the door to you and your ex-boyfriend making out. Hot and heavy, I might add.'

Her cheeks flushed. 'These are…recent occurrences.'

'Are they?' Summer's voice was dry.

Autumn sighed. 'If I were a better sister, I would have known.'

'Ah, so that's it.' Summer picked up her tea. 'Missing this makes you feel inadequate.'

She blinked. 'How did you know?'

'I'm your sister,' Summer said, sticking out her tongue. 'Honestly though? I've seen you try, all your life. But no one expects you to be perfect.'

'Mum and Dad do,' Autumn said softly, the words slipping from her lips.

'What?'

She swallowed, tracing a finger along the outline of the mug. 'I've spent a good portion of my life trying to be perfect so they would notice me.'

'I… *What?*'

She lifted her shoulders.

'Autumn, I had no idea.'

'Why would you? It's what I've always done.'

'But why didn't I—?' She broke off. 'Okay, first off, this feels like we've done a role reversal. I'm wondering why I haven't seen any of this and you're telling me it's okay that I didn't.' She shook her head. 'Second. Wind, why do you think they don't see you? They love you.'

'Of course they love me. They just prefer you.'

'Why do you say that?'

'You were the one who was groomed to take over from Dad. They always asked about you. Everyone preferred you.'

There was a shocked silence. Summer shook her head.

'Dad groomed me because I had more of an aptitude for the business.' Summer tilted her head. 'Though he probably regrets that now.'

'Because you didn't end up there?'

'No,' Summer said with a small frown. 'Because you've got a successful business and you did it without much help.'

'He gave me the start-up cash,' she pointed out.

'He doesn't care about money,' Summer said with a wave of her hand. 'He cares about skills. Abilities. Look at how he groomed Wyatt. Wyatt had nothing but skill and ability. Money isn't a factor for Dad.'

Autumn wondered what it meant that Hunter had said the same thing.

'I think Dad had a very narrow idea of who you were,'

Summer said contemplatively. 'He saw your talent in the kitchen and thought you'd only be good at that. I'm sure he expected your bakery to be a small operation, not the juggernaut it currently is.'

'Wait—did you just say Dad saw my talent in the kitchen?'

'Yeah. Mum and Dad. Why else do you think they kept asking you to create things for their parties? They wanted to show you off.'

'But—'

'And if you're talking about Mum asking about me, it's because she was worried about me. Trust me,' she added with a shake of her head, 'parents don't talk about their easy children as much as they do their harder ones.'

She squeezed Autumn's hand.

'Then you said everyone prefers me?' There was a pause. 'Please don't tell me you're talking about Timothy Rogers again?'

Autumn wanted to shake her head, but she ended up nodding instead. Summer rolled her eyes. 'He was an immature jerk for asking you to the dance. Probably still is. Now, what else do I need to poke holes into so you'll believe you're a formidable woman?' she asked with a wicked smile.

Autumn tried to smile back, but her sister's claims had her head spinning and nothing she wanted to do with her face seemed to be happening.

It was strange to hear Summer's account of her life. Strange—though that didn't feel like the right description—how Autumn had used the same experiences Summer had positively recounted as negative reflections on her character. She'd had a fear and fed it so often with examples she'd framed with blinders on that it had grown and taken over her life. Her relationships. Her views of family.

A clear example of it was her bakery. She'd been so disappointed that she hadn't been chosen to run Bishop

Enterprises that she didn't see the support her father had given her with the bakery. She hadn't even allowed herself to see that things had turned out exactly the way they should have. She had her dream job. The bursts of creativity she had while designing her pastries or a wedding cake fed her soul. Running the café fed her mind. And she was damn good at them both.

Seeing that, saying it, even in her mind, loosened a knot in her stomach. Her hand lifted to it, acknowledging it. That knot had been there as long as she could remember. Would it change anything now that it was gone?

'I'm sorry you had to deal with all this alone,' Summer said quietly. 'I know what it's like. It sucks,' she added without skipping a beat.

Autumn laughed. 'Well, we are twins. I suppose that means we'll share the same experiences.' She hissed out a breath. 'You don't have to apologise. This isn't your fault.'

'Ditto.'

'You know,' Autumn said after a moment, 'I used to feel so invisible around you.'

Summer's cheek lifted in a half-smile. 'Funny. I used to feel that way about you.'

'You did?'

'Not to the extent that I'd try to get Mum and Dad's attention,' Summer clarified. 'But I remember thinking, not that long ago, actually, how much better you would have dealt with it if you'd been the one to find out about the affair. If Dad had asked you to keep it a secret.'

'I would have done the same thing you did.'

'That's not true.' Summer shook her head. 'You know how to deal with things instinctively. You don't struggle. You just…do.'

She saw the truth in that. Linked it to what Hunter had said about giving people what they wanted. Before, she'd seen it as a flaw, but maybe it was a strength.

'Why didn't you tell me?' Autumn asked.

'Because *I* don't know how to deal with things instinctively,' Summer said with a smirk. 'I struggle.'

'How did you think you were dealing with it?'

'Poorly. I knew that. I wanted to tell you, but I suppose...' Summer sighed. 'I was trapped by my own fears. It meant I needed to trust someone and I wasn't sure I could after what happened with Dad.'

'But that's in the past now, right?' Autumn prompted. 'Because you know you can trust me.'

'I didn't even know you were struggling,' Summer replied softly. 'I should have.'

'The point was that you didn't.'

Summer smiled. 'I'm getting there. I'll get there.'

Autumn reached out and squeezed her hand. 'Me, too.'

She felt better now that Summer knew everything. Not having to hide it any more took some of the pressure off. She was glad they were on the same page about what had happened to Summer, too.

She shook her head. 'We were idiots for keeping this from each other.'

'Yeah.'

'But we're okay?'

'Of course.'

'And you and Wyatt are...'

Summer's face turned dreamy. 'Great. It's nice to talk with someone you love.'

'I know.'

'With Hunter?'

'With you,' she said dryly.

'Oh.' Autumn smiled when Summer's expression turned disappointed. 'Well. I'm here whenever you want to talk.'

'Thank you.'

They drank their tea in silence. When Autumn finished hers, Summer let out an impatient breath.

'I'm here if you want to talk about Hunter, Wind.'

'I don't.'

'You're just going to let me wonder about that kiss—and that *baby*—without getting details?'

She studied her sister's face, and decided she'd kept secrets for far too long. 'It's his baby. He's a father.'

'What?'

Pleased with the reaction, Autumn began to tell her sister the story.

CHAPTER FOURTEEN

IT HAD BEEN three hours since Hunter had dropped Autumn off and experienced the kind of embarrassment he actively tried to avoid. But that wasn't the reason he was still thinking about it.

He could still taste and feel her. It was probably good that they hadn't been able to make love. He could only imagine how his body would have betrayed him then. How the memories would have killed him. But at least he was thinking about something other than Eli's cystic fibrosis test the next day.

It was happening the next morning, ten o'clock, and his stomach was churning from the worry. If his son was sick, he knew what kind of life Eli would have. The growth problems, the stomach issues, the respiratory symptoms, the daily therapy. Depending on how sick he got and how quickly, he'd be in and out of hospital. They'd have to be extra careful in public areas because he'd be more susceptible to germs. He'd never have a life like a normal kid, and Hunter would have to watch his child suffer in the same way that Janie had. And his length of life might be just as short...

He closed his eyes against the pain.

Opened them when the doorbell rang.

He wasn't expecting any visitors. The only person who would arrive at his house unexpectedly—his mother—was in Greece. He swung open the door, distracted by his thoughts, and blinked.

'Autumn?' he asked, shock tightening his throat. 'What are you doing here?'

Her eyes went from his head down to his toes. He resisted the urge to shuffle his weight. He was wearing an old T-shirt, track pants and no shoes. He'd changed as soon as he got home, figuring he'd spend the day walking Eli up and down the house and wanted to be comfortable. Since it was his normal work-from-home outfit, she'd seen him in it countless times before. So why did he feel naked now?

'You can change, right?'

'Yeah. Wait. What's happening?'

She walked past him, giving him a whiff of her perfume. He shut the door before the wind could take it away, desperate—slightly ashamed—to have something of her.

'I'm here to distract you.'

'What? Why?'

'I was being selfish earlier,' she said, avoiding his eyes. 'I shouldn't have left. I said I'd help and then I got into my own head—'

'Autumn,' he interrupted. 'You don't have to do this if it's hard for you.'

She stepped forward and cupped his face. 'I know.' She stayed there long enough for the heat to scar his face, then stepped back. Took another step back, too, as if the first hadn't taken her far enough away. 'You've dealt with losing Janie alone for far too long. Your mother leaves every year and your father's never really been here. With Eli…' She shook her head. 'You don't have to be alone with Eli.'

He opened his mouth, but nothing came out. He hoped she saw his answer, his thanks, on his face. The way she blushed, bit her lip and looked down at her boots made him think she did.

She looked cute, he noticed, though it was the wrong time to. She wore ankle boots and a white summer dress. A denim jacket hung over her handbag at her side. He wanted to throw her over his shoulder and take her to his bedroom.

'I don't know what to say,' he rasped. From emotion and desire.

'You don't have to say anything.' She looked around. 'Where's Eli?'

'Sleeping in his room.'

Her eyebrows rose. 'Without you having to drive some-where first?'

'Yeah.' He ran a hand over his head. 'I think he's as ex-hausted as I am. Now that I'm not freaking him out, he's probably feeling it.'

'Or maybe you're finding your rhythm as a father.'

He angled his head, accepting her comment though he didn't believe it. It had been five days, four of which had gone poorly. He'd need every one of the days before Grace got back to find his rhythm, and then he'd need a new rhythm.

An unexpected panic fluttered in his chest.

'How are you going to distract me?' he asked, to dis-tract himself.

'It's a surprise.' She threw her jacket and handbag on the couch. 'We have to wait until Eli wakes up, so if you want to do some work or catch a nap yourself, feel free.'

'I don't think I'd be able to sleep.'

'So do something you haven't been able to in the past week,' she suggested.

'Like what?'

She shrugged, went into the kitchen and began opening his cupboards. He had no idea what she was looking for, but when she looked at him, she quirked a brow.

'You can't think of one thing?'

'Gym,' he said, flushing. 'I'll go to the gym.'

She waved a hand and continued her search, and he moved to his home gym. His muscles ached by the time he was done. Probably not his best idea considering he didn't know what Autumn had planned for the night, but he had no choice. It allowed him an escape from his thoughts. An added bonus was that it helped him not to go into the kitchen and try to get Autumn to help distract him. Heaven knew where that would lead. He did, too, and he *liked* it.

Yeah, the gym was better.

When he walked into the kitchen after his shower, he

got a waft of sweet warmth that immediately made his mouth water. His eyes widened when he saw the batch of cookies on the table, before they settled on Eli, who was gurgling contentedly in his bouncer. There was a clank beneath the counter and then Autumn was standing, setting a brand-new batch on a cooling rack.

'Oh, hey,' she said, smiling sweetly. 'I didn't hear you come in.'

He grunted, annoyed at what her smile did to him.

'I hope you don't mind that I kept busy,' she continued, as if he hadn't been grumpy with her, gesturing to the cookies. 'Two batches of chocolate chip and peanut butter cookies. I know they're your favourite.'

'Where did you find the ingredients?'

'The shop. You didn't have anything,' she said indignantly, 'and Eli was still fast asleep, so I ran out.' She brushed a curl from her face. 'He hasn't been awake for that long, but I have fed and changed him already. I also packed a bag. He's good to go. Are you?'

His gaze had been following the curl she'd brushed away, which had joined the rest in a wild halo of hair around her face.

'Am I okay?' he asked, feeling a little jittery.

She tilted her head in question. He dipped his own, gesturing to his clothes. Her eyes sparkled.

'You're fine. We're not doing anything that requires a certain dress code.'

'You never know.'

'You do know. I just told you.'

'You said that the last time, too,' he replied darkly.

Her laugh was light and happy. 'Are you still mad about that? It was a social media challenge, Hunter. No one cared about your T-shirt and shorts.'

'If I'd known you were going to film me, I would have put more thought into the outfit.'

'But you didn't, and look how well it turned out!' she exclaimed. 'I promise there'll be no filming tonight.'

He narrowed his eyes.

'And you're dressed perfectly appropriately for what we're doing.'

'Which is?'

'Nah uh, you're going to have to wait and see.' She came around the counter, her eyes fluttering over his jeans and shirt. 'You look nice,' she said, sincerely.

'So do you.'

She smiled. 'Look at us. Two nice-looking people going out for the evening.'

His mouth half curved. 'Let's go before you say something stupider.'

Or before *he* responded in a stupid way. Like kissing her.

She took her keys from the counter, then walked back into the kitchen and checked that the oven was off. As she did, he stole a warm cookie, savouring the delicious heat of it. He finished that one, put a second in his mouth before retrieving Eli's pram and putting the go bag in it. He finished eating and took Eli out of the bouncer.

Autumn was watching them when he turned, and she offered him a small smile. Then she covered the cookies with a net he had no idea whether he'd owned or she'd bought. She was leading him to his car not long after since Eli's car seat was already in it, a cookie in her own hand.

He didn't recognise the route she drove. But he took advantage of the moment and Eli's quiet gurgles to close his eyes. He wouldn't sleep, but his mind was too tired to think. For the remainder of the trip he was able to rest, only opening his eyes when the car stopped.

'Here we are.'

'Mini golf?'

'Putt-putt,' she corrected.

He just looked at her.

She wrinkled her nose. 'You're not thrilled with this?'

'I'm...surprised.'

'Why?'

'I don't know. I thought you'd do something less...' He trailed off, unsure of what he wanted to say.

'Well, it's no more, no less,' she said after a moment. 'It is what it is.'

He smiled. 'That made no sense.'

'No,' she agreed with a sniff. 'But it's too late to take it back. Come on.'

They got out of the car, and she gestured in front of her. 'Welcome to paradise, my lord.'

He laughed softly, though he agreed with her assessment.

The mini golf course had been built on a beachside promenade that stretched between Mouille Point and Sea Point in Cape Town along the Atlantic Seaboard. There were children screeching in the park nearby, and couples already playing on the large course. People jogged and walked along the beachside paving; others sat on the benches on the lawn, enjoying the view.

The sounds all mixed with the waves crashing against the side of the promenade, flowing over and crashing against rocks that stood out in the ocean. The sun was beginning to lower in the sky. It added oranges and yellows to the blue, and with the wind gently blowing, it did feel like paradise.

'Thank you, milady,' he replied, turning towards her. She quirked her eyebrow, asking if it would suffice for the evening's entertainment. He nodded.

'Then let's go get some tickets.'

The game went by faster than he expected. It could have been because he was dividing his attention between Eli and watching Autumn. She was much more interesting than trying to earn points, though he tried, urged on by his competitive nature. But as soon as his turn was over, he'd pay attention to her again.

He liked that she was talking too much. It meant that she was nervous, or trying to distract him. Or both. It pleased him immensely. She chatted about the bakery and how they'd had to decline requests for wedding cakes because they were stretched so thin.

'I know I have to hire more people,' she said, bending over her putter. The wind swept past them, lifting the skirt of her dress slightly. He purposefully averted his gaze. 'But that feels like a task that'll keep me from doing more.'

'It will for a while.' He watched her ball slide past the hole. 'You're busy. Successful. You need more support. Doing it now will help sustain your business long-term.'

'You sound like my father.'

He stiffened, remembering how their conversation had gone the day before. 'He knows business.'

'He does.' She considered her ball thoughtfully. 'So do you. It's probably time I listened.'

He blinked. 'Yeah,' he said slowly, wondering how far he could push it. 'In fact, you're probably in a good position to think about expansion.'

'As in, expanding the bakery itself?'

'As in, expanding the brand,' he replied, relaxing as amusement spread through him. 'Different branches. Or having the wedding cakes be a separate business to the everyday of the bakery and café. Different staff, and you can oversee them all. That kind of thing.'

She didn't reply, and they continued their game. He won, though he was fairly certain it was because she was distracted. Since it distracted her from noticing him watching her, too, he didn't mind.

He couldn't help himself. His mind, his heart were demanding he memorise every inch of her face. They were afraid the chances to do so would be ending soon, though he had no evidence to prove that. He only had a feeling in his gut. A growing, pulsing feeling that felt very much like the panic he'd experienced earlier when he'd thought about Grace returning.

So he'd remember how she tilted her head from side to

side as she considered the ball. When she didn't, he knew she was thinking about what he'd said. He noted how she'd suck in her lip when she was waiting for him to finish his turn. How the wind blew her curls around her face; how she brushed at them without a second thought. And the smile on her face whenever she checked on Eli. Protective and content. As if Eli were hers.

As if he were *theirs*.

Hunter had meant it when he'd told her that: he did wish he'd conceived Eli with her. Seeing her take care of Eli—of him, too—though it had only been the last two days, had awoken that fierce need inside him. It almost overshadowed his fears; but thinking that immediately caused them to flare again. They pointed out that his genetic code hadn't changed. That his reluctance to have a broken family was still there.

The possibility of losing her was there, too. Then again, that seemed to follow him around regardless of the nature of their relationship. What else could that feeling in his gut be? He was dreading the moment they were no longer in each other's lives. It seemed inevitable. Now he realised it always had been.

Nausea rolled in his stomach as he thought about it. He didn't want to not have access to her beauty, her quirks. She drew his attention. Hell, she drew everyone's attention. He saw the way people looked at her. Something deep and primal would beat inside him every time he noticed their interest. Unashamedly, he'd look at them until they saw him watching, enjoying it a little too much when they scurried off in embarrassment.

As he thought of it, his heart twisted on itself. Begged him to make the aching stop. To leave her behind before she could leave him.

The thought paralysed him for a full minute. Even when his body had started moving again after they'd got drinks and food from a nearby vendor, his mind felt frozen.

'What's wrong?' she asked. She'd finished her hot dog already, and was now holding Eli, patting him on the back since he'd started to get fussy.

'Nothing.'

'Hunter.'

He finished his hot dog. Took a long sip from his soft drink.

'Tomorrow.'

It was all he said.

'Do you want to postpone it?' she asked tentatively. 'Maybe a bit longer after the anniversary—'

'No,' he cut her off. 'The sooner we know, the better.'

'Of course,' she murmured. Silence stretched, then she said, 'What was the worst part of Janie's illness?'

He stared at her as his mind went from frozen to gushing water. He got up, threw the empty can in the bin. Sat back down and threaded his fingers together.

Those days seemed like such a long time ago. A different life. A different version of himself. He'd been so scared of Janie dying. He'd done everything in his power to keep her alive. And then she'd died anyway.

The same thing could happen to Eli.

'Thinking she'd get better.'

She lowered to the bench slowly, still patting Eli's back as she rocked back and forth.

'I'm sorry.'

'You were right,' he said, eyes on the sky and its rainbow of colours. 'I can't let go of what happened to Janie. It'll always be something I carry with me.'

'No one's asking you to let go of it,' she replied, surprise clear in her tone. '*I* wasn't.' Her hand stilled on Eli's back, then the patting continued. 'The past is important to who we are. I just don't believe it should be more important than who we can be. Or what we can have.'

He didn't reply. She exhaled.

'I see now how hypocritical this was of me,' she said. 'I expected you to want to work through your past when I didn't want to work through mine. Not let go of,' she clarified, 'but…acknowledge, at least. The best-case scenario is to work through it, I guess.'

'What was I supposed to acknowledge?' he demanded quietly as his stomach burned. 'That my sister's illness made me afraid of having children in case they got sick? That my parents' fighting made me worry that that would happen in my relationships, too?' His throat was tightening now. 'I did that. I told you that.'

'Yet I only found out yesterday that her illness and your father's response to it made you afraid you'd be a bad father. Or that there's a part of you that blames yourself for her death.'

He blinked. She continued more gently.

'You said the worst part of taking care of Janie was hoping she'd get better. Last night you said you were scared of her dying.' She tightened her hold on Eli. 'I think you believe you could have done something to make her better.' Her voice softened. 'Or to keep her from dying.'

She was right. That was the fear rattling around inside him. The fear he couldn't identify.

'And we never fought, Hunter,' she added. He thought she might be wanting to distract him from that bombshell. 'If we argued, we resolved it quickly enough for you not to worry we'd end up broken.'

'But we did,' he said automatically.

'Because there was one thing we couldn't resolve. This.'

'You don't understand.'

'Exactly. That's my point.' Eli gave a little whine, as if sensing the tension. Autumn stood again. 'I did the same thing,' she told him. 'I never told you I felt as though I had to please people. My entire life I felt second best to Summer and it changed everything about me. *I* changed everything about me so I could feel like I was enough.'

He didn't understand how she could ever doubt that. And felt guilty that he hadn't seen as much of it as he should have.

'You are, Autumn. You're more than enough.'

Her lips curved. 'I'm trying to believe that. I can see that I should, anyway.' She paused. 'When we broke up, I didn't see it or believe it. I thought you thought I wasn't good enough to have a family with. He—' she nudged her shoulder forward, gesturing to Eli '—felt like proof of that.'

She continued before he could say anything.

'I also didn't see until recently that part of why I left was because I knew I'd always come second after your past, Hunter. You're not willing to move on.'

Surprise hit him square in the chest. 'I made you feel second best?' He shook his head. 'Because my sister died?'

'That's not what I said.'

'But you think it's a choice,' he ground out. 'That carrying this pain, this guilt is—'

He broke off when it all became too much. When he finally acknowledged the guilt. When his eyes burned, and his throat sharpened. He didn't like it. It felt too much like the vulnerability of the night before, and they were in public now. He couldn't cry in front of strangers.

'I know it's not a choice,' Autumn said, moving forward and shielding him against most people who were looking. 'Our break-up was because of my issues, too. Clearly. I was so focused on how inadequate I felt and the anger I had at my family for making me feel that way—' She broke off with a little breath. 'It hid the real issue, which is that I have low self-esteem.'

There was a pause, as if she couldn't believe she'd said it. Then her eyes met his.

'Maybe your anger at your father—and worrying about your genes and repeating your parents' relationship—is doing the same thing.'

'The guilt?'

She smiled at him sadly. 'I can't answer that for you, Hunter. But you don't have to figure it out now.' She looked down at Eli, then moved to pick up his bag. 'Come on, let's go. Your son is tired.'

CHAPTER FIFTEEN

HER CONVERSATION WITH Summer had reminded her how important it was to have support. She'd immediately thought about Hunter, and how his mother wasn't home and how Grace wasn't nearby. She knew he wouldn't ask Ted to come over and keep him company. She also knew that spending time alone with Eli would only remind him of what was coming the next day so she'd driven to Hunter's place.

She didn't need her mental voice to tell her it wasn't her responsibility to distract him. But she wanted to offer him support. She was his friend and that was what friends did. A lie, that voice had said, and she'd accepted it as such. She preferred not to think of the motivations for it.

Her plan had been putt-putt and dinner. It hadn't included the cup of coffee she was currently making them. Nor had it involved a conversation where she bore her soul and got nothing but turmoil in return. A part of her ached at that, though she wasn't sure what it had expected. A miraculous realisation of just how stuck he was in the past? And how selfish did it make her that that answer was yes?

'You know,' she said, because talking was better than thinking, 'that expansion plan is interesting. I bet I could ask my father for advice. It would likely bridge some of the gap.'

She walked over to the couch, handed him the coffee. When she reached down to the biscuits she had placed there earlier, she saw a significant portion of them already missing. She hid her amusement.

'That's a surprise.'

'I know,' she replied. 'But if I want to move away

from the anger, I need to acknowledge my mistakes.' She winced. 'That wasn't a dig at you.'

'I didn't think it was.'

She smiled. He smiled back.

And for the longest moment, it felt as if nothing had gone wrong between them.

'Do you think your father knows about this distance?' he asked, sipping from his coffee. The action looked deliberate.

'I don't know,' she admitted. 'Based on the conversation I had with Summer, I don't think so. None of them knew how I felt.'

'Neither did I.'

In that, she knew he was telling her there were things about her he hadn't known either.

'That was deliberate,' she answered. 'I didn't want you to know I felt inadequate. Partly because I didn't want you to notice it, and see all the flaws that feeling that way made me so familiar with. And partly because it in itself felt like a flaw. A weakness.'

'You felt like this throughout our relationship?'

She nodded. 'For most of my life.'

'How didn't I see it?' he asked accusingly; he wasn't accusing her though. Then he blinked and met her eyes. 'Have I been *that* focused on my own stuff?'

She didn't know how to reply. Another consequence of a lifetime of people pleasing was a desire not to hurt their feelings. But her silence told him what he wanted to know anyway, and he slid into his own thoughts, not drinking his coffee, not eating the biscuits.

She knew what he was feeling. She'd felt that way the night before, seeing him cry. The realisation that their relationship hadn't been as good as they'd thought before its end was jarring. The fact that the other person had been hurting and they hadn't seen it, painful.

It made her want to distract him again. But the idea she

had to do so was bad. Terrible. It would probably make him angry again. She took a moment to consider whether it was worth the risk. Her eyes swept his face—his tight, miserable expression.

Screw it.

She got up, got his phone off the counter. She searched for the relevant song on the Internet, connected to his speakers, and pressed Play. When it started, he looked up.

At least it was soft enough that she wouldn't wake Eli.

'What are you doing?'

'Teaching you how to do this properly,' she said lightly. 'It's been bothering me for ever.'

'You didn't seem to have a problem when you put it on the Internet.'

'No, I didn't,' she agreed. 'But that's because part of your appeal was how poorly you danced.'

A deep rumble sounded from his chest. With delight, she realised he'd growled at her. *An actual growl.* Fortunately, she wasn't stupid enough to let him see her amusement. Though she was tempted.

'Stand up,' she commanded him.

'No.'

'Fine,' she said, and began to do the ridiculous social media dance he hated right in his line of view.

He watched her without expression, even as she did the moves wildly, more ridiculously. When that didn't even make him smile, she began to improvise, adding in sounds and moves that grew more terrible as she went along. He didn't respond at all, and she narrowed her eyes, stopping.

'You don't find me entertaining?' she asked, offended.

'I do. Just not now.'

She didn't believe it. She was always, without fail, able to cheer him up. Even if for a moment. She blamed her next actions—her next terrible, *terrible* actions—on the unexpectedness of being unable to amuse him.

'Okay.' She kicked off her shoes, pulled off her socks. 'I guess I'm going to have to play dirty.'

'What are you doing?'

'What do you think I'm doing?' she asked irritably, throwing off her jacket. 'I'm distracting you.'

'You're...'

His voice faded when she pulled her dress over her head. His eyes widened, and his entire face contorted in surprise—then desire. She didn't bother taking off her underwear. It wasn't necessary, and she was pretty sure it would get her into more trouble than she was bargaining for if she did.

'Your pool is probably at the exact right temperature now, isn't it?' she asked nonchalantly, dragging open the glass doors that led out onto the patio and yard. She grabbed the baby monitor off the table, hoping Eli wouldn't wake up soon. 'I bet it is. Do you mind if I go for a swim?'

She directed the question over her shoulder. He was still sitting. Still staring. She almost laughed, grateful for her choice in underwear that evening. The red colour did wonderful things to her skin, and the lace accentuated the curves of the body she'd learnt to love.

He finally noticed her looking at him, and his Adam's apple bobbed as he shook his head.

She kept her smirk for when she turned around, placing the baby monitor onto the grass before diving into the pool. The water was a shock of cool at first, and her body braced against it before she relaxed and surfaced. When she did, she realised it was pleasant, as she'd predicted.

She kicked her legs, pushing a hand against her curls to get them out of her face. She would regret wetting them so late in the evening later, when she got into bed and realised the thickness of them had retained most of the water. It was worth it though, she thought, remembering the look on Hunter's face as she'd stripped.

There was a splash and the water rippled. She stopped thinking about it.

He surfaced metres away from her. Close enough for her to see desire still simmering on his face; far enough that he couldn't do anything about it.

Yet.

'No,' she told him shakily. She cleared her throat. 'I mean, we're not going to make out in this pool.'

He smiled. 'I know.'

'You do?'

'Yes,' he replied solemnly. 'It would only lead to me making love to you on the ground next to the pool.' She gaped at him. 'If you're lucky, I'll take you to my bedroom.'

'I was going to offer to stay over tonight,' she said once she'd found her voice again. 'Now I'm thinking that might not be a good idea.'

His face sobered. 'Nothing will happen if you don't want it to.'

If you don't want it to.

He was putting this decision in her hands. She'd literally jumped on him earlier that day, and he was forcing her to make this decision. Which was probably why he'd done it, she thought, and almost smiled.

'I don't,' she said softly. 'It wouldn't be a good idea if we did.'

'You didn't think so earlier.'

'That was before I spoke with my sister.'

Summer had been sympathetic to her situation, but she'd warned Autumn to be honest about what she wanted—and what she could have. She wanted Hunter. She knew it. Was tired of lying to herself about it. But she also couldn't have him. Sleeping with him wouldn't make accepting that, facing it, any easier. So she wouldn't.

'Remind me to send her a thank-you note,' he said darkly.

'You should,' Autumn said with a laugh. 'Trust me,
this is a path we shouldn't go down.' She swam closer to
him, putting her hands on his shoulders. 'You know that,
Hunter. It's easy to forget when we're like this. Alone in
the dark. Under the night sky.' Her hands lifted to take his
head. 'So we'll have to settle for this instead.'

'What's this?'

She plunged his head under the water before he could
finish asking.

It was a while later that Eli's cries drew their attention. They'd worn themselves out playing in the pool like
kids, and when they got Eli settled again, Hunter spread
a blanket on the grass. She'd accepted a long-sleeved top
from him, which was enough cover for her for the warm
night. They lay under the stars, his head on her belly, her
hands behind her head.

She was more relaxed than she'd been in a long time,
regardless of the circumstances. Things seemed simpler
in this moment, just as she'd told Hunter. So simple, she
allowed herself to run her fingers through his hair.

'Hunter,' she said after what felt like for ever.

'Hmm?'

'Whatever happens tomorrow, you're going to be okay.'

He looked up at her. She brushed the hair from his
forehead.

'Eli's going to be okay, too,' she added softly. 'Because
he has you.'

'And you?'

She blinked against the heat that suddenly burnt in her
eyes. 'And me.'

They'd fallen asleep on the grass. Some time during the
evening, Eli's cries had woken them up. Hunter had waved
Autumn off to bed, telling her he'd take care of Eli. It was
a compulsion to do so, his mind and heart wanting to spend

the last hours before the test with Eli in case it irrevocably changed their world.

He hadn't slept much after that, and the next morning he and Autumn got ready in silence. She wore the same clothes as the day before, and her hair was tied up this time. He missed the curls around her face, but he didn't say it. He didn't say much of anything until they reached the hospital. Even then.

He felt as if he were in a different world. Lights were brighter, people moved slower. The only thing that anchored him was Autumn, at his side. Then Eli, who he took and held and murmured to in comfort. He was comforting himself just as much as he was his son. More than, because the kid had no idea what was happening.

Hunter held Eli as they went through the testing. He'd been tempted to hand over the task to Autumn, but he remembered that his actions mattered. He wouldn't hand over his responsibilities to someone else, no matter how hard they were.

And this was hard.

First, they performed the sweat test so they could check the amount of chloride in Eli's sweat. Some kind of chemical was put on Eli's arm, before an electrical stimulation was applied to encourage his glands to produce sweat. He started crying immediately, and Hunter had to actively stop his fingers from clenching.

Autumn shifted closer. It helped soothe some of his tension, though he could feel hers. The next forty minutes were spent in the hell of waiting, of wishing they could take Eli's place. The kind of hell Hunter had experienced multiple times before with his sister.

And look how that ended.

He pushed away the unwelcome thought as they moved on to take blood samples. He'd asked that Eli be tested for the cystic fibrosis gene as well. He wanted Eli to have all the information when he grew up. Even hoped he'd be able to prepare Eli in a way his own parents hadn't done with him.

Eli screamed at that, too, and it was a relief when everything was over, though there was still a tense silence when they left the hospital building. It was punctuated only by throaty little moans Eli gave at sporadic intervals.

'That was...intense,' Autumn said when they got into the car. She sat in the back with Eli. It was almost routine now.

'Yes.'

'Are you okay?'

He shrugged, because in all honesty he didn't know. He called Grace on their way back to the house, speaking to her on Bluetooth and explaining how everything had gone. She'd asked him to call her right away, but he would have anyway. If the positions had been reversed, he would have wanted to know as soon as possible.

When they pulled into his driveway, they sat in silence for a moment, neither of them moving. Eli had fallen asleep, exhausted by the trauma of the day.

'I know you have to get back to the bakery,' Hunter started.

'I don't.'

'You don't?'

'I've taken the day off.' There was a short pause. 'Is it too late to get something to eat?'

More relief poured into his body as he gave a small laugh.

They agreed on takeaway Thai so they wouldn't have to drive again. Eli woke as they took him out of the car, and Hunter fed and changed him before settling him in his bouncer. He fussed, but apart from that, the rest of the day was remarkably easy.

By early afternoon, Eli had quietened enough that Autumn took him outside. When they saw how much he seemed to like it, Hunter spread out the blanket they'd fallen asleep on the night before again. He brought Eli's things closer, before going inside and getting himself and Autumn something to drink. Then he watched her.

She played with Eli effortlessly, as if she'd been made to do it, though he was too small to do anything but watch and occasionally gurgle and smile. He loved her excited squeal whenever that smile came. Loved when she told him the object of all her games was to elicit that smile. She eagerly offered to feed Eli, and his heart melted watching her do so.

He'd known long before then that he was still in love with her. He'd made excuses, told himself it wasn't relevant. But he didn't bother with that now. Now, he let the love touch the deep and damaged parts of his soul.

And was afraid of how much it healed them.

CHAPTER SIXTEEN

AUTUMN GOT THE call two days later at three in the afternoon.

'He's not sick,' Hunter said when she answered, forgoing the hello.

She put her hand to her mouth to prevent a sob from
escaping. She was standing in front of the counter, visible
to her entire bakery, and the small noise she made caught
the attention of a few clients.

'Hold on,' she told Hunter.

She went into the kitchen to tell Mandy she was taking
a break, ignoring the look of concern she got in return.
She'd explain later, she thought, keeping her head down and
walking out of the bakery. She only stopped when she was
at her house. As she sat on the recliner at the patio, she let
out a breath of relief. Hunter was still on the phone, waiting.

'I'm so glad to hear that,' she said shakily, not bothering to hide her emotion. 'You must be so relieved.'

'I am.' There was a pause. 'I really am.'

His voice cracked at the end. Autumn thought her heart
did, too. She took an unsteady breath, then another, and
another, until finally she couldn't fight the tears.

'Are you crying?' he asked.

'No.' She sniffled. 'Why would you think that?'

'No reason.'

She could hear the smile in his voice.

'Does this mean he doesn't carry the gene either?'

'We'll only get the results of that next week.'

'That's enough for now.'

'It is.' He waited a beat. 'Can you make a celebratory
dinner?'

'I...'

She trailed off as logic caught up with her. Now that the testing was over, she had no real reason to go. She'd stopped lying to herself, which meant facing that they didn't have a friendship. They were clinging to each other because their relationship was special, but being Hunter's 'person' would only bring her heartache. She should wean herself off.

'I don't think that's a good idea,' she said with a constricted throat.

'Okay.'

The single word was ominous, and held more emotion than anything Hunter could have said.

'It's not… We shouldn't…' She let out a harsh breath. 'I'd have to leave now, Hunter,' she said lamely, settling for her professional responsibilities when the personal ones to herself didn't seem to be working. 'I can't leave closing up to Mandy again.'

'I understand.'

She closed her eyes. 'Do you?'

He didn't say anything.

'Hunter… I'm as relieved as you are about Eli not being sick.'

Which bothered her. She'd grown too attached to the baby. She wanted to say it was like those times when she'd been younger and pretended to be a mummy to whatever she could find. But she knew it was more than that. The emotion in her heart was too bright, too big to blame a game of pretence. Even more concerning was that she'd spent all of three days with Eli. Barely that. What would happen if she invested more time?

'I can't abandon my responsibilities,' she finished softly.

'We'll see you some other time, then.'

'Hunter—'

'I wanted you to know he wasn't sick,' Hunter interrupted. 'I didn't call to put you in a difficult position.' He paused. 'I didn't want you to worry.'

'I appreciate that. I really do.' Despite all of her logic about why she shouldn't get involved, the fact of it had her saying, 'Screw it. I'll be there.'

'What?'

'I'm coming to celebrate, Hunter.'

She wasn't sure how she knew he was grinning, but it had her grinning, too. And ignoring how, deep down, she knew she was making a mistake.

That one night of celebration morphed into something else altogether. Making that concession had led to making a million more. Autumn could blame no one but herself. She wanted to spend time with Eli and Hunter. Found herself drawn into the allure of their makeshift family. And all the while she knew she would pay the price for compromising on protecting herself.

She didn't think of that as she spent weekends at Hunter's, playing with Eli. Enjoying how he was growing; how he'd begun to trust them. After a month, she and Hunter had settled into their own routine. Autumn had found herself giving more responsibility to Mandy at work, and had finally hired additional staff to assist with the bakery's demands. She spent all her free time with Hunter and Eli.

Hunter had relaxed since Eli's test results had come back negative, more so when the blood test had confirmed Eli wasn't a carrier of cystic fibrosis either. He'd taken the relief of that news and channelled it into getting to know his son. He changed nappies and heated milk like a pro, though her favourite thing was listening to him speak to Eli about his work. As if the little boy could understand and help his father with the problem of renewable energy.

Since she made fun of Hunter because of it, Autumn would never admit that sometimes she wondered if Eli did understand. When his big brown eyes were so intent on what Hunter was saying. Or when he occasionally 'talked back' in the form of burps or gurgles. Hunter clearly en-

joyed it when his son did those things, and was as atten-
tive and intuitive a father as Autumn had always known
he would be.

If she'd spent any time thinking about it, she could have
anticipated how witnessing Hunter's transformation into
a parent would make her feelings for him grow. But she
was too distracted by playing house. Even as she began
to see it, to feel it, she resisted it. Resisted how sexy, how
enthralling she found watching him take care of Eli was.

She ignored the danger, too. Autumn knew it long before Summer warned her.

'Wind, why are you doing this to yourself?'

'I'm not doing anything,' she said defensively. 'I'm…
being a good friend.'

Summer snorted, sticking a fork into the cupcake she'd
ordered at the bakery. Summer had told Autumn she ate
a cupcake with a fork to keep from staining her fingers.
Autumn had retaliated that it was a mark of a psychopath.

'Is that what you're lying to yourself with?' Summer
asked. 'You're not his friend, Autumn. *You* told me that.
And now you're co-parenting Eli?' Summer frowned,
shook her head. 'What happens when Eli's mother gets
back? When there's no reason for you to spend all your
time around Hunter?'

Autumn didn't reply, though she met her sister's gaze.
Summer's voice softened.

'What do you think is going to happen when he realises
you're still in love with him?'

'I'm not—'

Summer silenced her with a quirked eyebrow.

'Okay, fine.' Autumn said, with a little huff. 'I know
what I'm doing.'

Summer looked at her sceptically. Autumn was forced
to agree. Because she really, really didn't know what she
was doing. The last time she had, she'd told Hunter she
needed space. Hours later, she'd been at his house.

A part of her was waiting for him to choose her. She knew she was waiting in vain. It was the same thing that had happened towards the end of their relationship. She'd waited and waited, her insides shrivelling up more and more as she'd realised he wouldn't choose her.

But they'd both changed, the waiting part of her offered. She could sense it in herself. She'd left some of the anger behind. Felt more of it fade as she allowed herself to acknowledge her gifts. As she set tentative boundaries for herself with people. Hunter had left his obsession with becoming like his father behind, too. He was also facing his grief, she thought, remembering the times he'd compared taking care of Eli to his experience with Janie.

It happened almost naturally, and they were almost always good memories. He didn't freeze at the mention of her name, though his stories usually ended with him getting a sad, distant look on his face. She would, without fail, lean over and brush a kiss over his cheek, then grab Eli's little arms and pretend he was speaking to his father. Hunter would laugh, and play with Eli, exactly as she'd intended. She wanted to draw him back to the present. To remind him he had something, someone to help with the pain.

Perhaps those changes in them had been the cause of her waiting. But the fact that she knew the outcome wouldn't change told her that she was fooling herself. More importantly, it had an annoying voice in her head asking if she had really changed when she was in the same position with the same man.

It asked the question as the weeks passed and she spent her free time with the Lee men. When her heart swelled to a million times its normal size every time she saw Hunter. As a rush of love and protectiveness flooded her whenever she saw Eli. And when seeing them together had her body going heavy with an emotion she had no words for, but instinctively knew was dangerous.

And then it happened.

The decline into coolness was gradual. Slow. At first, she'd thought nothing of the cancelled plans. She'd missed Eli and Hunter, but the bakery had been busy, so she had been, too. Something clicked in Autumn's head when he cancelled again though. And again, and again. When she hadn't seen them in a week, she knew.

She began preparing herself for what was coming.

It had happened without him realising it. One moment he'd been living his life, taking care of his son, enjoying the company of his person. The next he'd realised he was part of a family.

And he *loved* it.

The fear had happened as unexpectedly. Grace had mentioned on their daily video calls that she'd be seeing Eli in less than six weeks. *Six weeks.* His mind had taken the words and enshrined them; there had been nothing and no one that could distract him from it. Grace would be back soon. The life he'd settled into with his son and his person—his family—would soon be over.

All of it had shaken him so much he'd begun cancelling his plans with Autumn. First, he'd claimed he had the flu. Then, he'd stopped giving excuses at all. He didn't want to lie to her when he was bracing for what he knew was inevitable.

Loss.

It didn't matter that caring for his son had eased the burden of grief he still carried around about Janie. The helplessness he'd had no idea had contributed to his grief—his guilt—had faded because he *could* help Eli. He didn't claim to understand it, but being able to do things for Eli somehow made up for what he hadn't been able to do for Janie.

Perhaps it was that Eli could live the life Janie hadn't

been able to. And Hunter could be there for Eli in the way
he'd always wanted to with Janie.

It felt…powerful.

But what did that matter if he was about to lose his son?

The fear built and built, until he could see no way
around it. It was as if the barriers he'd fought to tear down
were back and closing in on him. Unsurprisingly, the feeling had him driving to Autumn's bakery. He got there
around seven, an hour after the store closed. The light was
still on when he arrived, and he tapped against the glass
when he tried the door and found it locked.

Autumn looked up from behind the counter. There was
a pause before she walked over and opened the door.

'Where's Eli?'

'My mum.' He felt a wave of shame and guilt for not
telling her. 'She came back on Tuesday.'

She searched his face, then nodded.

'I need ten minutes. We can talk after. Wait at the
bench.'

She closed the door again. After a brief hesitation,
Hunter went to the bench she was talking about. It was
a few metres from the store, and afforded whoever sat
there the stunning view Autumn had all to herself when
she went home.

The two of them would often share meals at the bench
when they'd been dating. If Hunter came over for the
weekend, he'd work while she was in the kitchen and
they'd take lunch there. Or he'd sit there for a moment of
quiet, and she'd bring him coffee as they watched the blue
sky, enjoying the barely perceptible buzz from the city.

Tonight, the sky was turning from light to dark blue. A
pink hue courted the clouds, merging with the orange of
the sun. In a few minutes, those colours would turn into a
navy darkness, a stunning backdrop to the stars that would
twinkle inside it. Hunter wondered what was wrong with
him that he thought it romantic.

Ten minutes later, she showed up at the bench. She didn't sit. He rose, faced her. She didn't speak. Just shoved her hands into the knitted jersey she'd thrown over her unofficial uniform of all black.

'How did you know I wanted to talk?' he asked, hedging his way into a conversation he had no idea how to start.

'Easy. We haven't spoken in over two weeks. It's your usual MO.'

He frowned. 'No.'

She rolled her eyes. 'You're right. You didn't do the same thing after I broached the topic of marriage when we were dating. We saw each other every weekend, every week for two years, and then you stop coming around, calling, answering phone calls.' She added with a detached tone, 'For two weeks.' She shrugged. 'This is almost identical.'

'It's not the same.'

'Right.'

The word dripped with sarcasm. It put a rod in his spine. Poured petrol over an anger he hadn't known was there.

'Okay. You're right. But I was dealing with things.'

Her expression remained stony. An illogical part of him lit a match, held it over the petrol.

'You're not going to ask me what?'

Her lips pursed. It was the only sign that she'd heard him.

'Autumn,' he said through clenched teeth. 'I'm trying here.'

'No,' she said. 'You're not. You're here because you need me.'

He opened his mouth. Closed it. Frowned.

She gave a mocking little laugh and turned on her heel. She was almost back on the path to the bakery when he found his voice again.

'That's it?' he called, his legs pushing him forward. 'You tell me I need you but you *walk away* from me?'

She'd stopped walking, but she only turned when he said that. Her expression was still carefully blank, but her eyes were fiery with emotion. He took a perverse satisfaction in that.

'Yes.'

She turned again, took another step forward.

The match dropped and a fire ignited.

'I knew I'd lose you some day, too.'

She stopped again.

'I thought you were different.'

She turned, her eyes ice.

'You're blaming this on me.' It was a statement. She tilted her head. 'I shouldn't be surprised. You still don't want to face the real issue, do you?'

'This again?'

'Why did you come here tonight?' she asked. 'Was it because you realised we were playing at being a family and you wanted your pretend wife to fulfil your—' her lips curved mockingly '—physical needs?'

'Don't,' he growled.

'So that's going too far?' Her voice had lost its edge now. It sounded curiously empty. 'You were fine with accusing me of being the one to walk away. Not to forget how you're ignoring that I would have given anything for us to stay together. In fact, I contorted myself in so many ways to be who you needed that I gave you *everything*.'

He opened his mouth but she ploughed on.

'So what do you need this time, Hunter?' She took a step forward. 'What did you come here for?'

'I don't want to lose you,' he blurted out, the surprise of her words creating a compulsion inside him to be as honest. With himself, too.

'You came here because you don't want to lose me?' she repeated.

It was close enough to the truth. He nodded.

'Why would you think you'd lose me?'

'It always happens.' Each word exposed more of himself. He didn't like it. He couldn't stop it. 'When Grace returns, everything will change. I'll lose you, and I'll lose Eli. I'll lose the family we had. We'll end up broken and I can't—'

He broke off when it felt as though there were no more air in his lungs. As if a snake had curled around them, and had gone in for the kill. When he fought it off and regained his breath, he looked at her and choked out his next words.

'I don't want to lose another person I love.'

CHAPTER SEVENTEEN

THIS MAN. THIS infuriating, complicated, *broken* man. How could she be angry with him when he said that? When he told her he was afraid to lose her? When he all but admitted he loved her?

Half of her had already crumbled into itself, falling at his feet and promising to do whatever he wanted. The other half was still angry with him. Furious, actually, because he'd ignored her for two weeks and now he needed her.

She listened to the angry half, because the other half was the old Autumn and she'd vowed not to regress when she'd been preparing for this conversation. The angry half apparently had control over her legs, and they propelled her into moving again. She was certain she would fall apart from the tension between the two halves soon. From the tension between wanting him, but also wanting more than she would ever get from him.

She deserved more.

It was a significant realisation. But the new Autumn accepted that she deserved what she wanted. She no longer believed she had to mould herself into someone else to receive her parents' love. Or to have a future with Hunter. She'd earned that by being there for them, helping them, supporting them. Like when she'd been there for her parents after the affair and they'd wanted to be a family again. Like when Hunter had come to her after finding out he was a father.

All of those actions had come from her. Because she'd wanted to do them. Because she was a good person, damn it, and good people deserved to feel wanted. They deserved to have people in their lives who treated them as if they were enough.

She loved Hunter, but she knew, even after his admissions, that he wasn't one of those people. She knew it *because* of those admissions.

So perhaps he had lost her.

'Did you hear what I said?' he asked, following behind her.

Without answering, she switched direction. She'd been going back to her store, but she'd already locked up and put the alarm on. Her house keys were in her pocket, and her handbag was safe in the bakery until the next morning. Besides, she needed home. The home she'd built. The place she'd created for herself. She'd mourn losing the men she loved there.

She'd mourn the time she'd lost by trying to be someone else there, too.

'Autumn. Autumn, damn it!'

She stopped when he jogged in front of her, blocking her path. When she tried to pass him on the left, he merely shifted his body. She didn't bother trying to go to his right.

'Get out of my way.'

'Did you hear what I said?'

'I did.'

'You don't have anything to say to me?'

She considered it. 'Yes, I do. I'm proud of you.'

A short silence followed. It told her he was surprised.

'Why?'

'This is your real issue.'

Another silence. 'Did you know?'

'Only when you said it,' she replied honestly. 'But it makes sense.'

'How?'

'No,' she said with a shake of her head. 'I can't figure this out for you.'

He exhaled. 'You're right.' There was a pause. 'I guess the thing with Grace is pretty clear.' She didn't answer.

Thought it best that he work it out for himself. 'I'm scared I'm going to lose Eli when she gets back.'

'Haven't you spoken about custody yet?'

'We said we'd do it when she gets back.'

She moved her tongue against her inner cheek. 'You could broach the subject now. It would help you feel better.'

He didn't reply.

'Look,' she said impatiently, though it was at herself because, despite her resolution, she was helping him. 'A woman who reaches out to the father of her child so she can pursue a career that'll allow for a better future for her son doesn't sound like someone who's going to run off with your kid.'

'I'll bring it up the next time we talk,' he answered after a pause. 'But what if—?'

'Hunter,' she interrupted. 'Are we done?'

She felt his gaze on her. 'I *have* lost you, haven't I?'

'That's what happens when you're careless with things.'

'I wasn't careless,' he said. 'I was *careful*. You mean so much to me and I didn't want my baggage to ruin that. Us.'

'So you didn't fight for our relationship,' she said slowly as the realisations just about fell on top of her. 'You didn't try to work through your baggage because you were afraid to lose me even if you did.'

'I pushed you away because I thought it would be easier. A choice.'

'Why did you come back?'

'It wasn't easier. I...needed you. And as friends—'

'There was less of a chance you'd lose me,' she finished. 'A bonus was that you didn't have to face your past to keep me.'

'Yes.'

She studied him in the silence that followed. Though she couldn't see the features of his face perfectly, she knew them like the back of her hand. As if she'd carved them herself. As if she'd created them.

She'd spent so much time studying that face. When they were dating, she'd just look at him sometimes. She'd enjoy how handsome he was. She'd enjoy his broody quietness that somehow elevated the lines of his face into something so striking it stole her breath.

Almost as clearly, she knew his emotions. His admission had cost him. He wasn't used to the vulnerability. He was worried about Grace returning. About the family they'd created. He was scared of losing it. Of losing Eli. Of losing her. After losing Janie, the fear was overwhelming. Eli had forced him to face the grief that he'd been running from for years. He felt raw from it, as if it were still fresh.

She wished she could do something to make him feel better. But that would mean assuring him he hadn't lost her, or them. If she did that, she'd be putting herself second. She couldn't tell Hunter to face his issues if she didn't face hers. And she didn't only want to face them; she wanted to work through them. So she couldn't revert back to old habits. She had to put herself first.

She would give him a chance to help her do so.

'You're an incredible father, Hunter,' she said slowly. 'Better than even I thought you could be, and I knew you had it in you.'

His ragged breath told her how much that meant to him. She couldn't let him enjoy it.

'I loved seeing that. I loved being there with you and Eli. I loved our little family.' She waited the briefest moment. 'It was always going to be temporary though. Eli isn't my child. You and I are just friends. We were pretending.'

'What if we weren't?'

'Do you really mean that?' she asked seriously, ignoring the hope. 'You're willing to take that chance?'

He stepped forward, as if he meant to assure her of it, but she shook her head. She wasn't sure he could see it until he stopped.

'I don't want you to say yes because you're afraid of losing me. I want you to say yes because you've realised being with me is more important than that fear.'

She put a hand on his chest, memorising the broad strength of the muscles beneath his fingers. She felt him trembling as she moved her hand from left to right. As she settled it over his heart.

'I love you,' she whispered to him, looking up. 'I know you know that. I also know you love me, too. But...do you love me enough?'

'I—I do love you.'

'That isn't what I asked.' She paused. 'I need you to tell me you won't let your fears control your actions. I'm not saying they won't influence them. And I don't expect you to toss them aside and forget they were there. But you can't relegate me into the role of a friend because you're scared of losing me. You can't opt out of taking care of your son because you're afraid you won't be a good enough parent. I need you to try. To choose me, and our family.'

'You make it sound so easy.'

Her fingers curled into a fist at his chest. 'This is the second time I'm asking you to choose me, Hunter.' She steeled herself. 'I won't ask you again.'

'I can't just let go of the fears,' he rasped, his hand covering hers.

'So you keep saying.' She stepped away from him, folded her arms when her hand wanted to reach for the warmth of his again. 'But I've seen you do it for Eli. You didn't shy away from him during the testing even though I know you were scared.'

'I...'

His voice trailed off, his confusion clear. She would have been more sympathetic, more patient if she didn't feel her throat tightening. If she couldn't feel herself beginning to pay for her honesty. For her bluntness.

So she pushed.

'Can you choose me, Hunter?'

'Can you get over what I did?'

'I already have,' she said, immediately understanding what he was asking. Understanding that he was lashing out, too. Diverting. 'I was hurt, but Eli... How can I blame you for Eli?'

She almost laughed at the ridiculousness of it.

'You wouldn't let me say it before, but I'm sorry. I didn't do it because I didn't believe you were good enough.'

'I know.'

And she did. For once, she believed him. He'd helped her to see that.

Oh, the irony of it.

'I want to choose you,' he whispered.

'I know.'

'What if—?'

He never finished the question. She soon realised he wouldn't. He was too afraid of the what ifs.

If he couldn't choose her now, after she'd bared her soul and asked him to, he never would. It was time to let go.

'It's okay,' she said carefully. 'You don't have to do this any more.' She took another deep breath. 'You can focus on being a good father to Eli. Don't worry about me.'

She walked past him, only pausing because he'd reached for her hand and gently pulled her back.

'Please...don't do this. I can't lose you.'

'You can't choose me either.'

She pulled her hand from his and walked to her house, opening her door and shutting it again without looking back. She made sure the door was locked, then pressed her back against it. The sobs came then. Wracking her body as she slid down to the ground.

CHAPTER EIGHTEEN

ALL THINGS CONSIDERED, Hunter's mother had taken the news that she was a grandmother in her stride. As he'd told Autumn, it had helped that he'd gone in with the information that Eli wasn't sick. Abby Lee had been visibly relieved at that piece of news. She'd been less impressed at the news that Autumn wasn't Eli's mother.

'I still can't believe it,' Abby said, settling on the couch with a cup of tea a few days after Hunter and Autumn had had their big conversation. Fight. Whatever.

He grunted.

'She was the first person you told,' his mother continued as if he hadn't responded so rudely, 'and she's the only person besides me who knows.'

'I would have told you first if you hadn't been—' he hesitated '—out of the country.'

Abby studied him. 'You mean, if it hadn't been the anniversary of Janie's death,' she corrected softly. 'But let's be honest, boy, you always would have told Autumn first.' She paused. 'She should have been the mother of your child.'

'Mother.'

Abby gave him a sharp look. 'I see right through you, Hunter. You're devastated by whatever happened between you and Autumn last week.'

He shook his head, but didn't correct her.

'Is it because you're a father to someone else's child?'

'No.'

The simple answer had a ripple of complicated emotions going off in his chest. It didn't cause it though. The emotions had already been poised, waiting to be set off from the moment Autumn had asked him to choose her.

The moment he'd opened his mouth and lost his voice. His ability to be courageous.

'Well, if she could swallow that…' Abby's gaze was still sharp, though her voice softened. 'What happened?'

He was tempted to confess everything. He wouldn't have to carry the weight of it by himself then. After all, now that he didn't have Autumn to share his life with, he'd have to find someone else to confide in.

The thought sent off another ripple in his chest, though this time it was of pain. He clamped his lips shut and shifted forward on the couch, setting his own coffee on the table. Randomly, he wished for biscuits. It was another hole Autumn had left in his life. She'd made sure his house had been full of treats in the weeks they'd spent together.

Damn it, he missed her.

'It has something to do with Janie, doesn't it?' Abby asked suddenly. She was watching him, her eyes searching his face in that intense way mothers had.

He frowned. 'I don't… No.'

'You're lying.'

'Yes,' he said after a moment. 'I lost her.'

'We lost her,' Abby said softly. 'I sometimes wonder what she'd be like now.'

'Stubborn.'

'Breaking hearts.'

They grinned at one another. It lasted longer than Hunter thought it would, and when it was over, it didn't feel as heavy as he'd expected. The consequence of sharing, he thought. Of ignoring barriers.

He considered it a moment longer, then said, 'I'm scared, Mum. I'm… I'm always scared.'

'About what?'

He told her. About his fears of turning into his father. Of being a bad father. Of having a family. He told her about how guilty he felt because of Janie. How afraid he was that he'd lose more people he loved. About his fears for when Grace got back.

He told her about how he'd lost Autumn because of those fears. He'd missed her pain, too obsessed with his own. How it was a pattern since he'd put his own feelings first when he'd found out about Eli, too. How he needed her, but had been paralysed when she'd asked him to choose her.

The words spilled out as if he'd been put under a spell. It didn't help that his mother sat patiently, listening without disruption. Her expression was unreadable, her posture relaxed.

There was a long silence when he was done, and nerves exploded in his chest, his mind racing with the possibilities of what she might be thinking.

'Have you been carrying this since Janie's death?'

'Probably before. It wasn't the most important thing then.'

Abby let out a breath. 'I have a lot of things to say about this. I'll say only a few of them now because they're important, and then we'll move on.' She set her tea down. 'You shouldn't have had to take as much responsibility for your sister as you did.'

'Mum—'

'No,' she interrupted him. 'Let me say this. I was overwhelmed and things with your father...' She exhaled. 'I'm sorry, Hunter. Janie wasn't your responsibility. And you were my responsibility just as much as she was. You shouldn't have had to go through this alone.'

'It's okay,' he mumbled, embarrassed that she felt the need to apologise. And yet...it helped.

'Right. Now that we have that out the way.' She smiled bravely. 'You protect yourself because that's what you saw your father do. It isn't a criticism,' she added. 'You had to because we didn't.'

'I don't blame you.'

'I know.' The smile was genuine this time. 'But you don't have to protect yourself for the rest of your life.'

'You don't know that.'

'I do,' Abby disagreed. 'Your fears don't control you, my boy. If they did, you would have run far away from Eli and the responsibility of raising a child.'

'I ran away from Autumn.'

'Probably because you had the option to,' his mother said contemplatively. 'You didn't have a choice with Eli. He depended on you. He forced you to face those fears.'

'So, what, I have to force Autumn into depending on me before I can face my fears with her?'

'If she told you she loved you, I think she already does.'

And he'd let her down.

'You're stronger than you think, Hunter. This doesn't have to define you. It doesn't have to keep you from having what you want.' She picked up her mug. 'I suppose you have to figure out what it is that you want, and how badly you want it. If that's Autumn, and you love her—' she gave him a look that told him they both knew it was, and he did '—your fear of losing her shouldn't be the cause of you losing her.'

She kissed him on the forehead and disappeared into Eli's room. Hunter silently thanked her for giving him the space. He stared at his mug, ignoring the coffee inside, trying to figure out how he felt.

The conversation he'd had with Autumn had left his mind in a shambles. His heart, too. Before he'd spiralled into the pit of his fears, he'd thought he'd been making progress. He'd started facing his grief more openly. He'd fully embraced being a father, and his experience in the first few weeks of being one—understanding his own father's reaction to an extent—had even had him thinking about reaching out to Calvin.

Even the family he, Autumn and Eli had formed hadn't

scared him that much, he realised now. The fears of bro-
kenness had faded.

When Grace had spoken to him about coming back
though, his instinctive reaction had burned up that progress and sent him back to the man he'd been before Eli had
arrived. That had been the man who'd driven to Autumn
on Friday night. A man desperate for his anchor. Whose
needs and fears were more important than anything and
anyone else.

It had even been that man who'd told his mother of
his fears, Hunter thought. Because as he worked through
it, he realised that some of those fears no longer applied.
About turning into his father, about having a broken family. Some of them he was facing, like his guilt about Janie
and what would happen when Grace got back.

He'd always been scared about being a bad father, but
that, he thought, remembering his mother's response to his
confession, might just come with the territory of being a
parent. As for his fears about losing the people he loved…
Well, as his mother had said, they were the reason he'd
lost Autumn.

She'd had every right to ask him to choose her. To walk
away when he didn't. Though it was of no benefit to him,
he was proud of her for doing so. He'd once asked her how
she planned on working on her issues. She hadn't had an
answer for him then. She'd more than made up for it now,
strong woman that she was.

He was so in love with her. And he'd be with her now,
if he'd followed her example and faced his issues.

But what if he did now?

The idea that he didn't have to be constrained by his
fears seemed too good to be true. Which told him he was
scared. Again. Despite the encouragement his heart was
giving him.

The night he'd spoken with Autumn, he'd heard the
encouragement. He hadn't been able to do anything then

because he'd been too overwhelmed, panicked by the idea of losing her. But he heard it now, and he wanted to pay heed to it.

He would have to adjust, of course. He'd have to learn how to move without the weight of his fears around his ankles. To navigate the world with his new freedom. He wanted his freedom to take him to Autumn. He wanted…

He wanted to choose her.

His legs were carrying him to Eli's room before he'd realised it.

'Mum, Eli and I are going to see Autumn.'

Abby smiled brightly at him, bobbing Eli up and down. 'Okay.'

'I'll be back before lunchtime.'

'Bring Autumn with you, dear. I'd love to see her again.'

'I'm going to try damn hard to.'

'Language,' she sing-songed, but smiled approvingly.

Eli smiled approvingly, too.

Hunter grinned.

CHAPTER NINETEEN

'AUTUMN!'

Mandy burst into the kitchen with enough force that Autumn's hand shifted and plopped frosting all over the cake she'd been decorating.

'What is it? What's wrong?' Autumn glanced over in alarm.

'Er...nothing.'

'Nothing? You burst into the kitchen like a maniac because nothing's wrong?'

'I came here because there's...' Mandy's eyes were disturbingly bright. 'You should come inside.'

'I'm not going inside if there's nothing wrong,' Autumn said irritably, turning back to the cake and trying to fix the frosting. 'I'm going to stay back here where I don't have to talk with anyone.'

It had been her strategy since she and Hunter had spoken. Keep busy, avoid people. Ignore the hole in her heart because she'd left a piece of it with him as she'd walked away. Mandy constantly hovered around her, having been privy to a brief overview of what had happened. Autumn appreciated the concern, though she wasn't able to show it yet. Only her annoyance.

'Well, there's a really cute guest here to see you.'

Autumn paused. 'To see me?' She let out a breath. 'Mandy, please don't tell me you've brought another blind date to the bakery. I told you, I'm not interested in—'

'Autumn,' Mandy snapped. 'Just come out here.'

Sighing deeply, Autumn put down the offset spatula, turning.

'This had better be good,' she said as she passed Mandy and walked through the door.

As soon as she entered the bakery, music began to play. She recognised the song. It was the one everyone had done the social media challenge to a couple of years ago. The one she'd tricked Hunter into dancing to. The one she'd tried to cheer him up with before Eli's test.

She tried to shake the memories off, knowing he was simply at the forefront of her mind. It was probably a co-incidence. Or the music had likely been playing all along and she'd missed it because she'd been concentrating on the cake.

Then she saw him.

She wasn't sure how she'd missed Hunter at all. He was standing in the middle of her bakery, ignoring the grins he was getting from her patrons. And he was dancing. Doing the moves as clumsily as she had when she'd been trying to cheer him up the night before Eli's test. Though it wasn't because he was trying to; rather, because he had a baby in his arms.

Her heart immediately turned into a puddle as she watched Hunter try and get Eli to do the moves with his limp little arms. Her eyes shifted over the room, where people watched gleefully, their eyes as bright as Mandy's had been. Then Autumn was looking at Hunter again, wondering why he was there. Trying to push down against the hope that had surged inside her at seeing him.

When the song ended, along with his terrible dancing, her customers clapped and cheered. She clapped, too, though her hands stilled when he walked towards her.

'Do you have a moment to talk to *#BakeryBoyfriend*?' Hunter asked softly, his voice breathless. 'Before you answer, consider that I come with *#BakeryBaby*.'

'How could I resist Bakery Baby?' she asked, amused. She held out her hands, quirking her brow in question. Hunter handed Eli over, and something settled in Autumn's heart as she held his comforting weight.

'I'm taking five, Mandy,' Autumn called behind her.

She followed Hunter outside, grateful for the warm day that prevented her from having to shield Eli from the wind. They walked until they were obscured by one of the trees close to the bakery, offering them privacy.

'Cheap shot,' she said, holding Eli tight against her. He rewarded her with a gurgle.

'I know.'

'Which is why you did it. The dance and bringing Eli with you.'

'Yes.'

'Why?'

'I would take any cheap shot if it got me points with you.'

'Why do you need points?'

'So you'd accept my apology.'

'What are you apologising for?'

He lifted a hand over his head, his expression wry. 'I guess I didn't earn any points then.'

'I didn't say that.' She kept her expression carefully blank. 'What are you apologising for? Why are you here?'

He took a long time to answer. Autumn used the time to cuddle Eli. She'd missed him, and she had no idea when he'd grown to be such a part of her. He wasn't even her kid. But she loved him, and her eyes burned at the idea that he'd grow up and she'd have no reason to be in his life.

Her heart burned that he'd grow up, and she wouldn't get the opportunity to see Hunter be his dad.

'You love him,' Hunter said after a moment. She blinked, and was relieved when she didn't feel the wetness she was certain was there fall down her cheeks.

'He's a baby,' she said, avoiding the question.

'Do you love all babies?'

'I…like all babies.'

Hunter gave her a patient look. It annoyed her. 'But you don't love them all.'

'No.'

'You love him, though.'

Her arms tightened around Eli. Lying felt as if she was betraying him. 'Yes, I do.'

Hunter's cheeks lifted, then he grew sober. 'I'm sorry for a lot of things when it comes to you, Autumn.' He paused, as if considering where to start. 'Mostly, I'm sorry for not telling you I choose you.'

'You don't have to apologise if that's how you feel,' she said softly, not meeting his eyes. A gasp passed her lips when he took her chin, lifted it.

'It's not how I feel. I wanted to choose you. I was just... I was scared.'

More air shuddered through her lips.

'Why are you here?' she asked hoarsely.

'I'm here to choose you.' His hand shifted to her cheek, caressing the skin there. 'I thought you were the most important thing in my life before you helped me see I was putting my fears ahead of you.'

His hand dropped and he squeezed his eyes shut. Opened them again. 'Something shut down inside me when I lost Janie. It didn't start again until I met you. I... I didn't know how to live with it. It was this...overwhelming love that made me want the things that had turned it off in the first place.' His voice lowered. 'The deeper I fell for you, the more I wanted those things, and the stronger the fears became. They were like a noise in my head getting louder and louder, and I couldn't hear you when you asked me to choose you that first time.'

'And now?' she whispered.

'Now... Now I see the noise kept me from hearing myself, too. I want you,' he said simply. 'I want the chance to listen to you now because I didn't before. I want to tell you you're the most amazing person and make you believe me. I want to see you face your issues and tell you how proud I am as you do.' A slow smile crossed his lips. 'I'm proud of you for knowing you're worth more than I was willing to offer you on Friday.'

He brushed a hand over Eli's head.

'I want you to be a family with me and Eli. We can figure out the rest as we go along.' He paused, and she saw the nerves on his face. 'If you can forgive me.'

She snuggled into Eli, then held him out and let Hunter take him.

'Are you saying this because you need me for something?'

'Yes.' There was barely a beat before he said, 'I need you because I love you.'

The lump in her throat that had been growing with his every word burst, showering warm emotion into her body.

'What about your fears?'

'I'm working on it,' he said dryly, and she remembered when she'd said the same words to him. Her lips curved. 'That's what I meant when I said we'd figure out the rest,' he continued. 'I have to work through them. But I know what my priorities are.' He pressed a kiss to Eli's head, his eyes heating when they met hers. 'You and Eli will always come first.'

She recognised his growth in those words. In the very fact that he was there. She didn't blame him for needing the time to figure it out, though she could have done without the heartbreak. But then, the heartbreak was necessary. Everything on this path had been necessary so they could be standing there in front of one another.

Her journey had been triggered when she'd found out the truth about Summer's experience. Realising what her issues had cost her with her sister had planted the seed. She had always been bound to face her anger and low self-esteem after that. Everything that had happened with Hunter, including walking away from him, had simply sped things up.

It had also been the growth of that seed.

As their gazes held, she felt as if it were finally blooming.

'I don't regret what we've been through, Hunter,' she said eventually. 'You shouldn't regret it either.' She waited a beat. 'Your fears have made you the man you are. If it wasn't for everything with your father, you wouldn't be as caring or as determined.' She hesitated only briefly before saying, 'If it wasn't for Janie, you wouldn't try to help people as much as you do. Or be strong for the people you love. Or try to protect them. Or love them so much you're afraid of losing them.'

His eyes flickered with emotion, but his gaze was steady.

'Does this mean you're accepting my apology?'

'You know I do.' Her heart shuddered, but she added, 'I love you, too.'

'I don't deserve you,' he whispered, putting his free arm around her. 'But I'm going to make sure you know our family is the most important thing. You'll never feel second best again.'

Autumn looked up, smiled. 'Damn right.'

She pushed up on her toes, her heart overflowing with love. But before she could reach Hunter's lips, Eli began to cry.

Their eyes met over his head, and they grinned.

EPILOGUE

Two years later

'IT'S NOT SO much that I wanted a holiday,' Autumn said casually, talking to the two-and-a-half-year-old straddling her stomach. 'It's that I deserved one, you know?'

Eli nodded solemnly. 'Holl-day,' he offered, reaching for something on the blanket Autumn was lying on. He handed it to her.

'Is this for me?' Autumn said, looking down at the marshmallow.

Eli nodded again.

'You're sharing?'

'Share.'

He took the marshmallow from her, and stuffed it into his mouth. Autumn laughed. Heard the deep rumbling of a laugh come from behind her.

'Dada.'

Eli clapped his hands as Hunter scooped him up.

'Yeah, buddy,' Hunter said soothingly. 'It's Dada.'

'Don't be impressed by that handclap,' Autumn said. 'He did the same thing when I ate a chip. It's his new thing.'

Hunter chuckled. 'I'm always impressed by what he does.'

'Helping him set realistic expectations for when he's an adult,' she said, pushing up onto her forearms. She pretended to steal Eli's nose, and he squealed with delight, clapping.

'Okay,' she said, wrinkling her nose. 'That's pretty cute.'

'So are you.'

Hunter stole a kiss, and after a moment, Autumn heard him offer to take Eli into the field. She lay back down as they went off. Hunter's deep voice vibrated, and Eli's cheerful laughter filled the air.

Autumn could have never imagined her life would change so much in two years. That she could be so content with it when once upon a time she hadn't even been happy with herself. Her thumb automatically stretched to her ring finger, where the ring Hunter had given her a year before sat solidly.

'Are you sure?' she'd asked breathlessly when he'd got down on his knee in the middle the flower field he and Eli were currently running in.

'I've never been surer of anything in my life.'

'I don't expect this of you.'

'I know.'

'We're already a family,' she'd said softly. 'I don't need—'

'Autumn,' he'd interrupted. 'What part of "I want to marry you" didn't you understand? It was a statement, followed by a question. A simple yes or no will do.'

'Hang on,' she'd said with a frown. 'I need to make sure you're okay with this. Because I don't need it. And neither do you.'

'But I do,' he'd said, his expression softening. 'I do need it. I want to call you my wife and make that commitment to you. I want everyone to know that I choose you.'

Her eyes had filled, and she'd said yes, and now they were planning a wedding. She was marrying the father of her baby. It might not have been her biological child, but Eli was as much her baby as he was Grace's. She couldn't believe there was a time she'd doubted it. Even Grace had freely concurred when Eli had called Autumn 'Mama'. Autumn had blinked in surprise, but Grace had said, 'Yes, that's your mama. And I'm your—'

'Mama!' Eli had shouted, and they'd all laughed.

Grace had become part of their family in the last two

years, too. She was funny and smart, and loved Eli more
than anything else. Autumn could have never anticipated
she'd be such good friends with the woman her fiancé had
conceived a child with. But that fact seemed so arbitrary,
so irrelevant to the nature of their relationship. Hunter,
too, had overcome his reservations about losing his son
once he'd started speaking to Grace about it. They'd figured out the co-parenting thing wonderfully, and Eli was
thriving because of it.

'Mama.'

Autumn opened her eyes to see the toddler's face a
breath away. She laughed. 'Hey, baby.'

'Fowers fo' Mama.'

'You brought me flowers?' She sat up, melting when
Eli handed her a bunch of uneven flowers from the field.
'Thank you, baby. Mama loves it.'

'Don't take all the credit,' Hunter said, grinning. 'I
helped.'

Eli looked unconvincingly at his father, before wad-
dling over to the marshmallows and eating another.

'Gosh, he's so big,' Autumn said, watching Eli. 'One of
these days he's going to be able to say words.' She turned
to Hunter. 'Actual sentences, I mean.'

'I know.' Hunter's eyes flitted to Eli, then rested on
Autumn's. 'We should start talking about the next one.'

Her breath caught. 'What?'

'We should explore our options.'

'I thought… What about…? But—'

'Autumn,' he interrupted with a small smile. 'You're
malfunctioning.'

She clamped her lips shut on what would have been
more incoherency.

She hadn't brought up having another child because
she thought she knew how he felt about it. Eli's existence
and health hadn't changed Hunter's previous concerns.
There was a chance their child could be sick. And if they

weren't sick, there was a chance they could be a carrier. Hunter wanted to avoid both those possibilities.

Though she had answers to his concerns, like letting herself be tested for the CF gene, genetic counselling or adoption, she was also content with their family. So perhaps she hadn't brought it up because it wasn't that important any more. She was already a mother. She was weeks away from being a wife. She had the family she'd always wanted.

'I don't need to have another child.'

He pulled her closer and she easily went to him, resting between his legs. 'What if I do?'

'I think you'd have to explain why. Is it because you really want one? Or because you think I want one? Or—'

'Is this going to be like the proposal again?' There was a faint whine in his voice. Autumn smiled.

'Not if you use your words and explain.'

'Okay.' There was a long pause. 'I can't tell you I want another child because I'm not scared any more. We'd have to do testing and depending on those results, we might have to talk about something else.' He paused. 'But I want Eli to have what I had with Janie.'

'He could get that through Grace. It doesn't have to be us.'

'Then I guess I want to experience seeing Eli with a sibling to look out for.'

'You could get that with Grace, too.'

'I want it with you.' His voice softened. 'I suppose all of this is selfish, then. You've proved to me that families don't have to be broken. You've helped me move out of the shadow of my fear that I'd be a bad father.' He kissed her head. 'I want to do this with you again.'

Her heart melted, but she turned to face him. 'As long as none of this is because of me.'

Hunter cupped her face. 'It's all me, baby. I want this. If you do.'

She studied him. 'I do.' He kissed her, and she shook her head when they parted, embarrassed by the heat at her eyes. 'It's disgusting how much I love you.'

'Good thing you're going to be my wife.'

'Good thing you're going to be my husband.' They kissed again. 'What a perfect life,' she whispered, and smiled.

* * * * *

LET'S TALK
Romance

For exclusive extracts, competitions
and special offers, find us online:

facebook.com/millsandboon

@millsandboonuk

@millsandboon

Or get in touch on 0844 844 1351*

For all the latest titles coming soon,
visit millsandboon.co.uk/nextmonth